RED SEA

DIANE TULLSON

ORCA BOOK PUBLISHERS

National Library of Canada Cataloguing in Publication Data

Tullson, Diane, 1958-
Red Sea / Diane Tullson.

ISBN 1-55143-331-1

I. Title.

PS8589.U6055R42 2005   jC813'.6   C2005-903271-5

First published in the United States, 2005
Library of Congress Control Number: 2005927692

Summary: After being attacked by Red Sea pirates, fourteen-year-old Libby
is left alone on a hostile sea, far from home, to fight for survival.

Orca Book Publishers gratefully acknowledges the support for its publishing
programs provided by the following agencies: the Government of Canada
through the Book Publishing Industry Development Program (BPIDP),
the Canada Council for the Arts, and the British Columbia Arts Council.

Design and typesetting: John van der Woude
Cover photograph: Getty Images

Orca Book Publishers
PO Box 5626 Station B
Victoria, BC Canada
V8R 6S4

Orca Book Publishers
PO Box 468
Custer, WA USA
98240-0468

www.orcabook.com
Printed and bound in Canada

09 08 07 06 05 • 6 5 4 3 2 1

For Brendan

Thanks to the usual suspects,
Shelley Hrdlitschka and Kim Denman,
and to Susan Goguen for
their help with the manuscript.

ONE

THE ROAD FROM THE CITY is paved but dusty, and my sandals atomize small clouds that sift over my pant legs, my
shirt, my chin and nose and eyebrows, then every strand
of my hair until I'm dun-colored and faceless. I can taste it,
Djibouti dust. It's like particles of people and animals and
African desert as old as anything is on earth, mixed with
crumbling plaster and car exhaust. I draw attention; anyone
new or different draws attention in these places, especially a
girl, alone. Not that it bothers me. Guys here are not much
different than guys at home. I know it bothers my mother
that I'm alone, and that's reason enough to do it. It's the

only time I have to myself, living on a sailboat with her and Duncan. I've seen walk-in closets bigger than our boat, but it could be the *Queen Mary* and still not be big enough.

Below me, along the seawall, the sailboats jostle at the dock lines, not so much from the breeze as from all the activity on the boats. It's pre-passage frenzy: crates of fresh food from the market stacked three-high by the boats, jerry cans of water and diesel line the seawall. We've waited here three weeks for the right weather for this Red Sea passage. Duncan's boat is moored near the end of the line. I can see him and Mom on the deck of the boat fussing with the mainsail. I can tell from the bony hunch of Duncan's shoulders that he's stressed. At his age, he should think about his heart. Mom stands next to him, trying to look like she knows what she's doing. She has more experience sailing than I do—about five days more. She took a crash course, so to speak, when they decided to take a year off from their college teaching jobs and fulfill Duncan's later-than-midlife crisis.

Two boats over, Emma is scrubbing the deck of her boat with a long-handled brush. She looks up, sees me and waves. It's not actually her boat. She and her brother, Mac, are delivery skippers. I like Emma. She's younger than most of this sailing crowd, twenty-eight, and she looks younger than that. She's wearing a ball cap, backward, and a bikini, her standard attire when she's working on the boat. Unlike the other women on these boats, Emma can actually wear a bikini. Slipping off my daypack, I rummage for the can of beans I've found for her, then wave it over my head. She shades her eyes to see, then gives me a thumbs-up. Emma likes beans for breakfast. She's British. She calls us Canadians *colonists*. Smiling, I head down to her boat.

She's dropped her brush and meets me on the plank suspended between the stern of her boat and the seawall. When I step toward her, she holds up a hand to bar me from the plank.

I say, "I'll take my shoes off."

She shakes her head. "You're all dust, Lib. You'll make mud."

"Well, I guess you don't want the beans very badly."

With a sigh she says, "Alright. But brush yourself off."

I do as she says, kick off my sandals and climb into the boat. Under the cockpit awning, the shade is cool refuge. I settle onto the cushioned bench and peel off my hat. "Why are you washing the decks when tomorrow they'll be covered in salt?"

Emma drinks from a water bottle, then tosses it to me. "I always clean the boat before a passage."

I empty the bottle. I never used to drink water at home. "So, it's some sailors' superstition?"

Emma flops down across from me. "Maybe. It's been lucky so far. Main reason though is that cleaning the boat is a good way to check things over. So, you found me some beans?"

I lob the can to her. She says, "Where did you find it? No, don't tell me. I don't care." She blows the dust off the top. "No bulges, no rust. Bonus."

"You'd probably eat them anyway."

She laughs. "Mac would."

We met Emma and Mac in Australia. Duncan bought his boat there, and Emma and Mac were picking up this one to deliver to Tel Aviv. In Djibouti we joined up with a couple of other boats to travel north, up the Red Sea to the Suez Canal and the Mediterranean. Mom wants to sail in Italy, the Isle of Capri and all that. Italy is still a long ways away.

I say, "Where's Fanny?"

Emma thumbs toward the side of the boat. "Feline terror. She dumped my basil plant last night, so we threw her overboard." She laughs at my reaction. "Put your eyebrows back, you know we didn't. She's sleeping. I rigged her up a basket hammock that she quite likes. Hopefully, she won't get seasick."

Fanny is a seawall kitten Emma and Mac adopted from here, one of hundreds that live off the town garbage. You never see an old seawall cat. I would have brought home a dozen by now except Duncan says he's allergic to cats. Right.

"Can I go see her?"

Emma feigns exasperation. "Who do you really come visit, the cat or me?"

"I brought you beans, didn't I?"

She shrugs. "I don't suppose you found chocolate?"

"On the next shipment from Paris, not that I could afford it anyway. I'd have to marry a Somali general and bear him ten brown babies."

"Steep price to pay even for chocolate, Lib, and it would only melt." She gets up and heads through the small door to the companionway below. "Come on, you can help me plot our course for tomorrow."

I follow her down the steps into the boat. "That sounds too much like school."

"Have you done any schoolwork today?"

"No, Mother."

Inside, the boat curtains are drawn against the heat of the sun. I blink as my eyes adjust to the dimness. "Although I did find an Internet café and read two newspapers from home. It's snowing there."

Emma shudders. "It always snows in Canada."

"Technically, somewhere, like the polar ice cap maybe. Not in Vancouver, even in winter. In Vancouver when it snows they close the schools. It's like a gift."

"And you checked your e-mail?"

I know what she's asking. She's asking if Ty has written me. It's almost three months now I've been gone. I e-mail him every day when we're in port.

I say to Emma, "I heard from my friend Jesse and she says Ty is moping." Actually, what she said is that school is boring and Mr. Waring, the PE teacher, is up on charges of sexual misconduct and that she has a new boyfriend, like that's news. "Ty is probably too sad to write."

The gray tabby kitten is curled asleep on a scrap of toweling in a round basket that Emma has suspended over the seating area. Emma rocks the basket gently. "She has the best berth in the boat." Reaching in, I gather the kitten into my hands. The kitten startles, then stretches and yawns. I cradle it under my chin. Emma says, "Fickle thing likes you best."

The kitten purrs as I stroke it. Some of the seawall kittens are too feral to hold. This one was born to live with people. "I'm going to miss you while we're sailing, Fanny."

Emma snorts. "We should be under a week to Port Sudan. I think you two can be apart that long."

I try to make my voice sound like I'm joking and say, "I could sail with you and Mac. I could be your crew."

Emma might laugh at the thought of me as crew, but she doesn't. "Your mother needs you. And Duncan does too."

The kitten rests its paws over my shoulder and gazes longingly at the top of the cupboards. When I scratch it behind the ears, it drools. "Mom and Duncan don't need me. They only dragged me on this trip because they couldn't trust me at home on my own."

"You're fourteen, Lib, never mind your gorgeous face and long red hair. I wouldn't have left you either."

"Right." She's been at sea too long. "I could have stayed with my dad. It's not like I would have been totally alone." Not that Dad was jumping up and down to take me. Every other weekend is more of me than he can handle. "I have an aunt, or my grandparents would have taken me." They would have, except they live a two-hour drive away from Ty, so what would be the point? "Duncan is probably endangering our lives."

Emma waves me off. "I'd sail with Duncan in a heartbeat. He's a flawless navigator, he maintains his boat in perfect condition, he sails better than a lot of racing skippers—"

I cut her off. "And I'd be fine on my own back home. Weren't you only a couple years older than me when you left home?"

Emma nods. "I was sixteen. But it was different for me." She pauses, looks at me. "Duncan seems to me to be a good man."

Now I snort. "So you win. *You* had the worst stepfather."

"I didn't mean that. You've got a different notion about Duncan. I'm just saying that I like him."

The kitten bats at a strand of my hair. "I have no idea what my mother sees in him."

Emma laughs. "Maybe he's good in the rack."

"Please."

"He's quite fit, you know, for someone his age. So limber." She lifts her eyebrows suggestively.

I set the kitten down on the floor where it proceeds to hunt imaginary prey. "Maybe you'd like to have Duncan."

She smiles. "Ooh, I might. I've always loved tall, dark, handsome men."

"Duncan is totally gray and wears glasses."

"Exactly right. He's nothing like my old boyfriends, and that has to be good." She laughs. "Why did you choose Ty?"

I shake my head. "I didn't. He chose me. Last year it was Taryn Talbot. Year before that it was Ashley Somebody."

"What, like a term position? He turns in the girlfriend with his textbooks?"

I smile. "He's not in school anymore, and any time with Ty is worth it, for as long as it lasts."

Emma rolls her eyes. "You're telling me exactly nothing about this guy. Let me guess, he has a car."

"He does, actually."

"And he's drop-dead gorgeous."

"He is."

"Bet he doesn't have a library card."

"He likes car magazines."

"Reads them for the pictures. Does he have engine grease under his nails?"

"No. And he chews with his mouth closed and doesn't scratch himself in public."

Emma nods. "Admirable, but you still haven't said what you like about him."

She's waiting for an answer. I say, "Everyone wants to be with Ty."

"And he's good to you?"

I look at her. "Of course he's good to me."

She says, "When I was sixteen, when I left my mother's, I went to my boyfriend's place. He always had lots of people around him too. One night he got drunk, more drunk than usual, and shattered my cheek."

"Nice. Sounds like a real winner."

"Well that's the thing, isn't it? Based on what my mother dragged home, I thought he was. Took me a while to see that I could do better."

Emma's looking at me, hard. I say, "What has this got to do with Ty? Just because the guy doesn't write me means that he's going to smash my face? Or has my mother been talking to you?"

"Your mother doesn't talk about Ty." Emma pauses. "It's more what I see in your eyes when we talk about Ty. It's like looking in the mirror."

Now I roll my eyes. "Right."

Emma scoops up the kitten and sets it on my shoulder. "But if you say that Ty is good for you, then I'll believe you."

The boat tips gently and I hear Mac's footsteps on the deck. He appears at the top of the stairs, a lidded plastic container under one arm, a net sack of lemons in his other hand. He grins at me and says, "Hey, Lib. What should I toss you, the lemons or the kitty litter?" He feigns a throw with the plastic bin, then passes me down the lemons. "All set over on *Mistaya*?"

"I guess." Duncan let Mom name the boat. *Mistaya*. Apparently it means *little bear*. I think it means *big mistake*. Still, I'll take *Mistaya* over the name on this boat: *Pandanus*. Emma says she doesn't name them, just delivers them. I take the lemons from Mac, set them on the counter, then the plastic bin. Examining it, I say, "This looks like regular sand."

Mac climbs down the stairs, his bare feet treading lightly on the polished wood. Mac is hardly taller than Emma and me, slim but well built, and his hair, even plastered with sweat, sticks out from his cap in blonde spikes. His grin gleams white against the tan of his face. "Not just any sand, I'll have you know. It's Sheraton beach sand, carefully screened to remove twigs or pebbles that might irritate the rich clientele. Or Princess Fanny." He strokes the kitten's forehead. To Emma he says, "I checked for cockroach stowaways."

Emma grimaces. "Keep the lid on, anyway."

Mac wipes his forehead with the sleeve of his T-shirt. Under his arms, the shirt is marked in half-circles of wetness.

But he doesn't stink, Mac; I detect just a faint scent of salt and sun as he leans close to me to pat the kitten. At twenty-four, he's too old for me, but he's nice to look at. He catches my eye and winks. "Pre-passage bash here at sundown. I'll save you a spot by me."

And a mind reader, apparently. I will myself not to blush as I hand him the kitten.

Emma jabs him in the ribs. "Chasing fourteen-year-old girls? Are you adding 'pervert' to your criminal repertoire now?"

Mac pretends to be hurt. "I've rarely, if ever, broken the law." He adds, "And got caught, that is."

I never know how serious Mac is being. Most of his so-called crimes seem to be fairly regular exploits, like when he was younger, downhill-racing in shopping carts. In Australia, I've seen him surf when there were sharks. No one else was anywhere near the water, not me, that's for sure. I don't even like wading in the sea. Swimming pools are bad enough, but at least in a pool you can see the bottom. Mac is fearless. In the towns we've been to, Mac explores the darkest lanes. He says that in hot countries, the shadows are the best places. Once, he took Emma and me into a tiny place, no tables, just a packed-earth floor, so dark I stumbled over my feet. We leaned against the plank bar and shared stewed lamb from a blackened terracotta pot, dipping bits of golden flat bread into a fiery broth of garlic and cumin that made sweat break out on my forehead. The proprietor gave us cans of warm Fanta soda, sliding careful glances over Emma and me before averting his eyes.

We always cover up before going into town, even our hair. But our eyes and fair skin are fascinating. I've stopped telling Mom where I go when I'm with Mac and Emma. I've stopped telling her much at all.

Mac hands me three lemons as I climb up the stairs. "Tell your mother I'm fond of lemon pie."

TWO

ON *MISTAYA*, MOM IS UP to her elbows, literally, in an immense pot of lasagna noodles. She always cooks for an army before we head out on passage so that she doesn't have to go near the galley for the first few days at sea. Mom gets seasick, Duncan too, although at least he can eat. I could cook, but they wouldn't like what I prepare, and with the motion of the boat, I might make a mess or spill boiling hot liquid onto myself. It doesn't matter. I'll eat the lasagna.

Duncan pulls his head from the engine compartment, wipes his hands on a paper towel and makes a note on a clipboard. To Mom he says, "Oil level is good." She murmurs "uh-huh," which is the extent of her interest in diesel engines. Duncan latches the lid to the engine compartment, then leans down to check the battery indicator. He's reminded me about nine hundred times: Always start the engine with one battery bank, let it recharge, then switch to the "house" bank to run lights, the refrigerator, and the electronics. That way you always have power to start the engine. No engine, no way to recharge the batteries. I'm not stupid, Duncan. Even on days with good wind, we always run the engine a while to recharge the batteries. And there are lots of days with no wind, or wind right on the nose, so that we run the engine just to get where we're going. Some purists sail without an engine at all. Duncan sees me and says, "Lib, can you mark off the list of spare parts as I call them out to you." It's not a question, and he hands me the clipboard. It's like a ritual with him, all this pre-passage engine checking, like a dog turning around three times before it goes to bed. I perch on the edge of the dining bench as Duncan lifts the lid to the locker. Inside, neatly labeled, is an array of brown boxes, zipper bags and bubble-wrapped lumps of machinery. I know it's all there. So does he. But we go through the exercise all the same. I show him the list, completely checked off, and he smiles, satisfied. "Check the go-bag, then, will you."

The red go-bag is a special waterproof vinyl bag strapped tight against the companionway. Basically, it's what you take to the lifeboat if your boat is sinking. It's a sacred pack of survival water, food and equipment, and we never use any of it, ever. I'm checking it now not to see that everything is there, because it is, but just to make sure the batteries are still good in the packages, that nothing has corroded or gone past its expiry date. Before each trip, either Duncan or I check the bag. Mom doesn't like to be reminded of the possibility of disaster.

It's heavy. I take the bag to the dining table and carefully unpack it. I know the contents off by heart, right down to the antibiotic capsules and the playing cards. Everything is double-bagged to keep it dry. In the bottom of the bag, my hand pauses on a photograph, also double-bagged, so that the image is shrouded under the layers of plastic. The photo is of Mom, Duncan and me, standing in front of the house not long before we left. The maple tree behind us is brilliant red, and there are leaves on the lawn. Duncan has his arm on Mom's shoulders and they're smiling. I'm standing with them, but not touching them. I'm looking somewhere different altogether, as if there are two people taking the picture, and they're looking at one person, me at the other. I don't remember, maybe that was the case. It's not a particularly happy photo, but I guess Mom didn't have a better one to put in. It's not like we were together often, the three of us. Or maybe Duncan put it in so that our bodies could be identified. I repack the bag, close it properly and fasten it in its place.

Duncan pours a glass of juice, hands it to me and pours another for himself. "The weather looks good, really, just a weak low-pressure area to watch, but we should easily beat it. It's the best forecast we're likely to get in this sea." He sips his juice. "So long as the forecast doesn't change, we'll get away in good time tomorrow."

I say, "I have to go into town again." I catch a look that darts between Mom and Duncan. "To mail schoolwork."

"You didn't do that today?" Mom's eyebrows are arched. She knows the answer, but still, she seems to feel the need to say, "You were to do that today."

"I have to finish one assignment. No point mailing part of an assignment. The stupid teacher will lose it and I won't get any credit."

"And you'd never lose it." Mom snaps a plastic lid onto a lasagna container. "I can't believe you didn't mail that stuff."

Duncan is quiet, placating. "You won't have time to go into town tomorrow, Lib. We're leaving."

I set my glass down, hard. "How many times have you told me that we're leaving? How many times have we dashed around like fools getting ready, only to sit around in port another week because the weather changed?"

Duncan says nothing, but a tiny muscle in his cheek clenches and unclenches. Mom says, "Don't try to deflect this. You didn't get the work done that you should have. It's that simple."

"I hate it when you say 'it's that simple.' Nothing is 'that simple.' I have to go into town. I'll be fast. Stop making such a case."

Mom slams down a plastic container of lasagna. "What are you really going into town for? To check your e-mail? To see if Ty has finally written you?"

I hate her now, I can't help it. Red-hot tears sting my eyes.

She continues, "When are you finally going to give up on that boy?"

Duncan steps in front of my mother. "Enough, Janine."

"I've got school to do." I toss my mother a look of pure hatred. "And I don't need *you*," I say, turning on Duncan, "to protect me from *her*." I unlatch my cabin door and bang it closed behind me.

"I DIDN'T MAKE a meringue because of the raw egg whites, even though the chance of salmonella is small; still, I wouldn't risk it, not before a passage." Mom's voice is singsong happy as she climbs under the cockpit awning, brandishing a lemon pie. "But we can top it with this," she says, waving a can of whipped cream with her other hand.

The others ooh and aah at the treat of a pie. Everyone has brought something to share, a potluck. So far I've seen chicken satays, a rice dish with nuts and a green bean salad. Emma and Mac contributed a loaf of golden-crusted herb bread that they baked in our oven, since Mom was already heating our boat to a zillion degrees with her lasagna. Mom hands Mac the pie like it's an offering.

He takes it, inhales the scent of lemon and sugar, and sighs. "You're an angel, Janine. An absolute angel."

She actually blushes. Has my mother no shame? To Emma I roll my eyes and she laughs. She says, "Can I get you two something to drink? Most everyone is just on juice and sodas tonight. Duncan?"

Duncan finally finds his way past my mother and her pie and takes a seat in the cockpit, as far from the kitten as he can get. Fanny winds herself through all the legs in the cockpit, mewing for treats. Emma hands Duncan a glass of juice. My can of Coke is just half-gone and already it's starting to taste warm. I slip past Emma through the companionway and down into their boat.

Emma has candles lit on the table and counters. She does this to save battery power, but the tiny flames soften the cabin and make for a cozy, inviting atmosphere. Mom won't have candles on *Mistaya* because she's afraid they might start a fire. Emma says candlelight attracts angels. Fanny has followed me to the top of the stairs and sits watching me. I break off a bit of chicken from one of the satays and toss it to her. She snags it and gulps it down. Once a street cat, always a street cat. Tonight I have to rummage in a locker for a bottle. The first I reach is Mac's scotch. He drinks his scotch neat, in a tiny glass. To mix it, even with ice, he says, is an abomination. I tip the bottle into my Coke can and listen to the glugs as it fills the can. I replace the bottle in the locker, throw the rest of the satay to the kitten and rejoin the others in the cockpit.

It's cooler now that the sun has set. The others are hunched over their laps with plates of food, the women clucking among themselves about their provisions for the passage, the men and Emma studying Emma's chart on the cockpit table.

Mac has probably sailed as many sea miles as Emma. They both used to crew on race boats, and they started their delivery business together. Still, Emma is the captain, and Mac seems content with his secondary role. Emma told me that the first thing she did after leaving home was to get Mac out of there too. She said her mother put up more of a fight over Mac. Of the boats gathered to sail the Red Sea tomorrow, Emma is the unspoken leader.

Emma indicates with her finger the fine pencil line on the chart, our proposed course for the passage. She had me calculate it today, taking into account dangerous reefs in the Strait of Lamentations, aptly named from my way of thinking. Some boats take several stops along the coast but we're sailing well offshore, the first of two passages to make the Suez Canal into the Mediterranean. Emma points to an area just off the penciled line. "There's potential trouble here," she says, tapping the chart. My mother glances up from her conversation with the women, her eyebrows suddenly creased. Emma sees this too and adds, "I mean the weather, from the low-pressure center. It seems to be stable, but we'll have to watch it. The weather can change so fast in this area."

Everyone nods, resigned to the inexact science of forecasting the weather.

Emma continues. "The winds will be with us for at least the first few days, as will the north-setting current, but then be prepared to motor against the wind. In either case, the seas will be short and steep. They always are, traveling north in the Red Sea. That means the passage will be choppy and wet."

"Like the inside of a washing machine," I say. "We should probably stay put."

Mom moans. "Will we ever get to Italy?"

Emma lobs a look my way. "It's up to each of you, of course, but I think we're making the right decision to go." She looks down at the chart, her finger again indicating the weather system below us. "It's a weak low, and if it moves faster than is forecast, or if we're too slow and it catches us, then we're in for a rough ride. But it's nothing you can't handle." She taps the chart along the African coast. "There are anchorages to hole up in, although threading the surrounding reefs presents a challenge, especially in weather, and you won't find much there in terms of habitation, a few huts on the beach, maybe, not exactly a pub for gin and tonics. Some anchorages are little more than desert islands, and you won't see a soul." She indicates the border area between Eritrea and Sudan, "Avoid this area, just to be safe. The politics here change like the weather." Then she taps the chart on the other side of the Red Sea, "Stay away from the Saudi Arabia coast altogether. It's closely guarded and they don't know your intentions. Stick to the fairway along the midline of the sea; that's your best course. The island of Masamirit is your target," she says, pointing to an island near the end of the penciled line. "Once you reach Masamirit, then it's time to head into the Sudan coast." She smiles at everyone. "I'm confident that a week or so from now, we'll be in Port Sudan toasting a successful passage."

A week at sea. Call it a passage, call it torture, sailboats must be the slowest form of travel. I swallow warm Coke and scotch and yes, it may be an abomination, but it creates the desired fuzziness. Fanny jumps up onto the back of the cockpit bench, pausing to investigate my ear. The kitten is pleasantly fuzzy too.

The men are still bent over the chart. I hear one mention *rebels*, which causes the others to mutter animatedly. Duncan looks up and checks my mother's face. I can see that she's watching the men, listening to them. Mac too looks up, then slides onto the bench beside my mother. The women fall silent.

Mac says, "We made it to Djibouti with no problems, didn't we? We're through the worst of it. Yes, there are trouble areas in these countries, but we're going to travel together, and most times we'll be so close we'll be able to see what each other is having for breakfast."

The women laugh.

Mac continues, "Small exaggeration, I know. Some boats travel faster, some slower, and you may not always be in visual range, but at the very least, we'll be in radio contact. We'll keep transmissions to a minimum and at low power, but everyone will monitor the emergency station. If a boat needs help, for any reason, you know we're close by."

A woman asks, "We won't use the radio to check in twice a day? We always do that," she says, nodding to her companions from another boat.

Mac shakes his head. "It may be over-cautious, but sometimes radio transmissions can be tracked."

My mother speaks, her voice tighter than normal. "What do you mean, tracked?"

One of the other women breaks in, "The rebels, don't you mean?"

"Or the military," a man, Jimmy, adds. "It's tough to tell one from the other. If they get your position from a radio transmission, they can hunt you down and rob you." His chin juts with self-importance. "Call them what you like, they're all just modern-day pirates."

My mother sucks in a breath, almost a gasp. "Pirates."

Duncan looks like he'd like to clobber Jimmy for uttering the word "pirates." He blurts, "Mac's right, we're sailing in a flotilla, we're sailing offshore. We're taking all precautions."

Mac raises his hand to stop Duncan's strident lecture. "The pirate attacks that we know about are almost without exception chance encounters—a sailboat being in the wrong place at the wrong time. These people aren't organized criminals, just hoodlums. Some are just fishermen seizing an opportunity. They might have a gun…"

"Fishermen have guns?" My mother has gone sheet white.

The volume in the cockpit is increasingly high. Mac raises his voice to be heard but stays calm, in control. He says again, "They *might* have a gun."

Jimmy snorts. "They *will* have a gun. An AK–47 Kalashnikov or something like it made in China, but an assault rifle, for sure. An AK–47 shoots six hundred rounds a minute. It'll cut a man in two."

Mac places his hand on Mom's shoulder reassuringly. "In some of these societies, men carry guns like we carry car keys. And knives too. They are cautious men living in difficult times. It doesn't mean they're going to harm you."

Jimmy sputters, "No, they just want to shoot up your boat and rob you blind."

Mac speaks to quiet the growing hysteria. "Fine, they'll *all* have AK–47s, according to Jimmy. I guess if one person carries a gun, it might be because everyone else does.

Expect that they'll have a gun, okay, but if they use it, they'll fire warning shots to intimidate you, not shoot up your boat." He gives Jimmy a look. "If you're faced with piracy, cooperate. Radio a mayday. Don't do anything to make the situation worse."

Jimmy is louder than Mac. "No one in these waters responds to a mayday. You read about that all the time in sailing magazines, how even commercial ships in this area ignore calls for help." Jimmy's face is red. His wife has her eyes lowered. Jimmy spouts on, "Like I'm going to invite the bastards aboard for tea. I'll blow the sons of bitches off their boat if they threaten me or what's mine."

Quietly, Mac says, "Or you could just let them have the stuff."

Jimmy doesn't seem to have heard. He's got himself puffed up, jabbing the air with his finger as he makes his points. I tip the rest of the Coke can into my mouth.

Jimmy's wife, I now notice, is much younger than him. A trophy wife, I wonder. Some prize he is. And imagine what he'll be like when he lives out his days in a recliner in front of the TV. Nice life for her. Maybe, when women marry these old farts, they hope the men will die young.

I guess my mother was a trophy too. Duncan stole her from my dad.

Emma folds up the chart, signaling the end of the evening. To my mother, she says, "We'll respond to a mayday, you know that. You won't be alone out there. And if it's any comfort, we're bound to have strong weather. That's sure to keep the pirates in port."

My mother attempts a small smile. "What would I do without you, Emma?"

"You'll be fine. You're well provisioned?"

Duncan blurts, "Provisioned? We have enough food for a month."

"Fuel?"

Duncan nods. "As much as we can carry."

Jimmy, his wife, and the others are gathering their things, saying goodnight. One after the other climbs down onto the seawall then makes their way to their boat. Duncan too gets up, as does my mother. Mac stretches his legs out on the cockpit bench.

Emma says, "What about books and diversions for the child?" She nods at me. "You should keep her busy navigating. She knows far more than she lets on."

Mom looks at me and the smile fades from her face. "Lib, are you not feeling well?"

"I'm fine." I'm halfway to my feet, wishing suddenly that I'd eaten something. It's a tight squeeze around the cockpit table, and I hang on to steady myself. "I'm just tired." Carefully, I place one foot in front of the other. Duncan reaches out his hand for me to take, but I wave it away. "I'm fine. Go on, why don't you?" Just as I reach the spot where Mac is stretched out, I stumble. With an ungentle oomph, I plant myself right on his lap.

I've surprised him, that's clear, and I'm pleased by his reaction. For a long moment, he doesn't move, then Emma says, laughing, "Mac, are you assaulting that child?"

He laughs, and so do Mom and Duncan. The thing to

do would be to get up, but instead, I say, "Just like an evil stepfather."

Silence drops like an anchor. Mac is on his feet in an instant, shoving me off him. Mom just stands there, her mouth opening and closing. Duncan has flushed so red that his eyes are watering. Emma looks from me to Duncan and back to me. "Lib, be careful."

I turn on her. "Excuse me? What did I do? Am I not the *child*? Are you saying it's all right, what he does to me when I'm asleep?"

Duncan is angry, I can tell by his tightly controlled words. "Lib, you are mistaken."

"You're a liar."

Mom holds her hands up. "We'll discuss this back at the boat."

I slap her hand away. "Oh yeah, we don't want anyone else finding out about him, do we?"

Duncan shakes his head. "Let it go, Janine." He steps down onto the seawall.

Mom apologizes to Emma and Mac. Mac won't meet my eyes. Emma gives me a long look. "Lib?"

Duncan stands waiting, watching me, his face concerned.

I turn away from Emma's gaze. "Forget it. I didn't mean anything."

"Lib, if you need to stay with us, you can."

"I'm fine. I don't know why I said that." I catch Mac's eye. "Mac, I'm sorry."

"I'm the one who should be sorry, Lib." He squeezes my hand.

Emma gives me a quick hug, says she'll talk to me in the morning.

I feel sick, and I know it's not just from the scotch. I climb down off the boat. I try to push past Mom and Duncan, but Mom grabs my arm. I could easily break free, but I let her speak. "It was the party, Lib. You know that."

Now I yank my arm from her. "Nice, Mom. Thanks so much for backing me up."

THREE

MOM STANDS IN THE COCKPIT of the boat, her hands on her hips, watching me. As I stroll toward the boat, Duncan emerges from the cabin, his reading glasses shoved up on his forehead, a folded chart clenched in his hand. When he sees me, his mouth forms a white chalk line. This morning, I waited in my cabin until they were occupied on the bow. They didn't see me leave. Neither did Emma or Mac; I made sure of that.

"You're late," Mom says.

I glance along the seawall. Emma and Mac have left, the others have gone and the empty spaces where their boats used to be remind me of teeth knocked out. The sun is already leaning to the west. I know not to bother looking to sea for the other boats' sails. They'll have been gone for hours. I am late. Very late. I decide on amnesia. "Late for what?"

I hear Mom take a breath. When she speaks, her voice is shrill. "I told you and Duncan told you that we were leaving today. It's all we've been talking about. You knew damn well…"

Duncan puts his hand on Mom's arm. "Get in and stow your pack, Lib. We're casting off." He spins and goes below.

Mom flings another volley in my direction, "We planned this Red Sea flotilla for weeks and now we'll be alone."

With a shrug I climb onto the stern of the boat, careful to scuff my sneaker on the painted letters of the name, *Mistaya*, then slip through the open transom into the cockpit. I squeeze past Mom without looking at her and into the companionway.

Below, Duncan is at the chart table bent over his electronic course plotter, transferring a coordinate onto a traditional paper chart. The main cabin never looks better than before a passage. The table and counter are clear, everything is put away behind locker doors, even the books on the shelves are held tight with bungee cord. At sea, nothing can be left loose to fly around. I set my pack on the counter.

Last night they stood at my closed door, talking at me until my silence forced them to give up. Now, Duncan is trying very hard to pretend everything is normal. So he looks at my pack and makes a fake "uh-hem."

"I'll stow it. I just need a snack."

I rummage in the fridge for some juice. Mom has the fridge layered with plastic containers of the pre-made meals. Not that anyone will feel like eating, anyway. I shove aside the containers and pull out a carton of juice.

"The lid."

Yeah, yeah, yeah. Save power. I let the lid slam closed. Duncan's glare prickles the back of my neck. I pull out a glass and pour the juice, then stand drinking it while I stare at Duncan. He's ignoring me now, penciling a line on his chart. His glasses are pulled down to the end of his nose. His gray hair is creased from the cap he wore today. Very attractive. Emma's right, he is fit, I have to give him that. He doesn't have the old guy gut my grandfather has, and Duncan is almost as old. Duncan is wearing jeans, an ancient T-shirt and his standard footwear for inside the boat: house slippers. I don't know how my mother keeps her hands off of him. I finish the juice and leave the glass on the counter. As I close myself into my cabin, I hear Duncan putting the glass away.

WHEN WE'RE SAILING, even though I'm stuck on the boat with them, I get more time and space to myself. Either Mom or Duncan is always in the cockpit keeping watch, and the other is often in their cabin, resting. They leave me alone. All that first night I stayed in my cabin, but today I made an appearance while Duncan was on watch. He asked me how I was doing, if I needed something to eat. He said that he was watching for the Zubair Islands, that he was glad we were passing them in the daylight, that sometimes the light-houses don't work and a sailor can run right onto the rocks. Then he told me about a book he was reading, a biography about a woman pilot in Africa before there were airfields. He said that back then pilots only flew in the daylight so they could see to land. This pilot, though, got caught out after dark, but her servant, who knew nothing about fly-ing but did know the depth of African night, lit fires along the landing strip so she could land. Then he told me about one of the Apollo 13 astronauts who as a young pilot train-ing in night flying from an unlit aircraft carrier, shorted out all his instrumentation and radio. He only found his ship from the phosphorescent trail of its propeller. Duncan started on another story, but I said thanks, that I got it, that lights are important if you're a screw-up pilot or astronaut. Fascinating, I said, that they lived to tell the tale. Yawn, I said, suddenly I'm ready for a nap.

Actually, I wouldn't mind reading that book about the woman pilot in Africa.

I'm hungry, so I make supper: soda crackers for Mom, warmed-up lasagna for Duncan and me. We eat in the cock-pit so that Duncan can keep his watch. We always stand watch when we're sailing, especially at night. Freighters and fishing boats can't always see sailboats. We need lots of time to get out of their way; a sailboat doesn't outrun any-thing. On passage, I usually stand one three-hour watch each afternoon, although no one called me from my cabin today so I didn't have to do it. Duncan and Mom do all the rest.

A white-winged bird buzzes the boat so close that I duck my head. The sea is still narrow here, and birds pass easily from Africa to Saudi Arabia. The bird dive-bombs again, narrowly missing the wire shrouds that hold up the mast. "Crazy bird!" Duncan follows my gaze to the circling flock overhead. The birds' movements seem tumbled and erratic, like socks in a dryer. Only Mom doesn't seem concerned that the birds have lost their minds.

The islands Duncan mentioned this afternoon are pale purple humps behind us now, or I assume it is those islands. It's not like the sea has signposts with arrows and mile markers. In sight of land we compare lighthouses and landmarks with those indicated on the chart to figure out where we are and check the GPS, an electronic positioning device, for our latitude and longitude. Even with the GPS, I'm always a little surprised that we find exactly the right entrance to a harbor. It's like finding a house address when none of the houses are numbered or the street signs are missing.

The faded islands are the only land I can see. Ahead of us, there's just water, the edge of everywhere and nowhere and only a pencil dot on the chart tells me we're anywhere at all.

As we eat, Mom's gaze never leaves the sea. I resist, I try, and then I ask her, "Watching for pirates?"

Duncan shoots me a warning look. Mom turns the color of toothpaste. "That's not funny, Lib."

Duncan unclips his tether from his harness and passes it to Mom. "Lib and I will wash the dishes. You stay up here." He gathers our plates and forks, and with a determined nod, motions me down the companionway.

Duncan washes, I dry. Apparently, I use too much fresh water when I rinse. He hands me a glass to dry. "I'd like you to stand watch with your mother tonight."

"Why? What did I do?"

That tiny muscle in his cheek clenches. "It's not a punishment, Lib. Your mother's stomach is upset from being at sea, she's not getting her rest when she's off-watch, and she's nervous. She could use the company."

I dry the glass. It has a label, the letter "J" for Janine. Duncan labels everything on this boat. I put away the glass. "You want me to fight off the pirates?"

Duncan sighs. "Your mother is entitled to be nervous." He takes a long time cleaning a plastic lasagna tub. "She has you to think about."

I barely hold in a snort. If Mom were thinking about me, I'd be home with Dad right now, watching big-screen TV and burning every light in the house. If Mom were thinking about me, she'd have let me stay at home too. But Mom isn't thinking about me. I say to Duncan, "Maybe you should stay up with her."

His hands pause in the sink. "I can't be awake all night, Lib."

I shrug. "Yeah, well, I was going to catch up on my novel study."

Clench. Unclench. Clench. If I'd tried that line on my mother, she would have launched a very long argument about how I should have used my time in port to get the assignment done, that I'm not managing my correspondence courses, that if I want to repeat ninth grade when we get back, then that's fine with her. When he speaks, Duncan is firm. "Just while we're in the southern Red Sea, Lib, I expect you on deck with your mother." He wrings out the sponge and leans on the sink. "Tomorrow or the next day, hopefully, we'll catch up with Emma and Mac and the others, and that will make your mother feel better. Right now we're not even in radio range." He looks at me, hard. "I don't expect any problems, but if you see anything, and I mean anything, out of the ordinary, you're to come and wake me."

FOUR

I POUR A CUP OF TEA from the Thermos in the cockpit, choosing the warmth of the drink over the real threat of having to pee while wearing nineteen layers of foul weather gear. Night watches are always cold, even in warm climates. I offer Mom the Thermos. She's standing at the wheel, nibbling a cracker with one gloved hand. The wind is light, and we're motoring with the mainsail. The engine is revved about as high as Duncan will allow for fuel conservation. Mom isn't wasting any time. She's tethered to the wheel post. I'm clipped on at the companionway, which means I can huddle on the cockpit seat under the canvas spray hood and stay out of the worst of the weather. Mom waves away the tea with a "no thanks."

"Of all of us," she says, "you're the one best suited to sailing. You never get seasick."

I slurp my tea and tip my face to the night sky. "I can't think of a place I'd rather be." In the dim light of the compass binnacle I watch my mother's face grow hopeful. The furrows in her forehead smooth out, a strand of brownish gold hair wafts against her cheek. When she was young, her hair was red, like mine. Her eyes brighten, hazel eyes that change from green to gray. My eyes. Mom smiles at me, and it reminds me of when I was younger, before Duncan, when it was just us. I start to smile back. But she should never have agreed to this trip. I say, "Unless that place was with my friends. Or my father. Or in an orphanage, if it meant I wasn't here."

Her smile disappears and she shakes her head. "You're not giving this trip a chance, Lib. When I was fourteen I would have done anything for this opportunity: a trip to Australia, then a one-year sailing journey to the Mediterranean."

"Through some of the most pirate-infested waters on the planet." I look pointedly at the handheld two-way radio dangling from her wrist and the arsenal of distress flares beside her in the cockpit.

She seems to ignore my comment, but I see her shoulders tighten and she scans the blackness behind the boat. "If you just let yourself, I think you'd enjoy this trip. You could learn so much. You could pick up your marks…"

"Don't start."

That stops her, briefly. "What I meant was, you're a good student, and without as many distractions…"

"If by 'distractions' you mean friends, then you're right. I don't have any friends."

"We have our sailing friends on the other boats." She extends her hand out into the night. "They're out there, Emma and Mac, the others. They'd do anything for us."

"They didn't wait for us."

"Emma and Mac hung back as long as they thought they could. You were too late getting back to the boat."

"Are you going to rant again about me being late?"

"You brought it up."

I hurl what's left in my mug overboard. "You like to think that this trip is such a good thing for me. But it's not about me, this trip. Not the smallest bit of it. This trip is all about you. Everything is about you. You and Duncan."

Her voice is quiet. "This trip is for us, Lib. I'm prepared to do whatever it takes to get us back on track. I don't ever want to feel like I could have done more. But I don't want to hear *anything* about Duncan." She takes a breath, pauses, then says, "You are so angry. For five years, you've been angry, ever since I married Duncan. You've made him into some kind of a monster, and he only wants what is best for you." I release one small guffaw. She says, "Duncan and I wanted to make this trip—"

I cut her off. "No. Duncan wanted the trip. You want what Duncan wants, so you went along. Thanks for dragging me with you."

"Let me finish. We wanted to make this trip with you, while we could, while there was still time to get your marks back up for university applications."

"Ha. You'll be happy if I finish high school. You took me because you don't trust me. You need to control my every waking moment and what better place than a floating bleach bottle half a world away from anything and *anyone* that's important to me."

She recoils after that last comment. Then she says, "You're important to me, to both of us."

"Both of us. You and Duncan. Duncan and you. Duncan who can do no wrong."

"Duncan isn't perfect, Lib, but you know he would never hurt you."

"And that makes me, what, the liar? Couldn't he be lying? Couldn't you be lying, just to protect him?"

This silences her, briefly. "Lib, Duncan is my heaven-on-earth, but I wouldn't protect him, not if he was harming you." She doesn't even blink. She pauses, breathes in, then says, "It's not that I don't believe you."

"How can you make those two statements? Don't they cancel each other out?"

Mom chooses her words as if she were picking up broken glass. "I think that you're confused."

"Oh, thanks very much. It's nice to know you have such faith in my mental capacity. Nice that my tea mug comes without a sippy lid."

"It won't hurt for you to be away a while."

"Away from what?"

"I've talked to you about Ty. You just don't want to hear me."

I make my voice mimic hers, "He's so much older than you, Lib." Then I say, "You marry a dinosaur, but Ty is too old for me."

She's losing her patience; her voice is clipped. "It's not just that Ty is nineteen, although I hate that he trolls for girls in the ninth grade."

"Trolls? You make him sound like a predator."

"It's not just me who thinks so. Lindsay told Denise that Ty is bad news."

Lindsay is my old best friend Vanessa's sister, in grade twelve now. Denise is her mother.

"How would Lindsay know?"

"Because she went out with him too when she was fourteen."

"No, she didn't."

"She did. For two weeks, then he threw her back and picked someone else. Apparently, he said she was 'too reserved,' although that might be Denise's euphemism."

Understatement, more like. Lindsay probably still covers her eyes in movies when people kiss.

I say, "Oh, so you're basing your opinion of Ty on Lindsay's two-week relationship?"

She inhales, her hands rest on the wheel as if it were a lectern or pulpit. "Nothing I've seen makes me think any differently."

Ty came to the door the first time we went out. After that, he said to watch for him and just come out to the car.

He never comes in if they're home. I say, "You don't even know Ty. *He'd* do anything for me."

I can see Mom wringing her hands on the wheel. Her voice is tight when she says, "Oh, I know Ty. I know him from that going-away party he threw for you at our house."

I say, "It was just a little party."

"We arrived home to police cars, Lib. We had to hire a drywall crew, and if that was the worst of it, then I'd be happy." Her voice starts to break. "You were so out of it."

I hardly remember that party. I change the subject. "You yanked me from all my friends. They'll ditch me, and you like the idea that I won't have any friends, any *distractions*." I turn so that she's looking at my back.

After a long time she says, "I just want us to be together, Lib."

"You should have thought of that five years ago when you left Dad."

Her voice softens and she says, "Lib, I really need for us to get along. I feel like I hardly know you anymore."

I get to my feet. "It isn't going to happen. Get used to that." I reach down to unsnap my tether. "I'm going to bed."

FIVE

I'M NOT SURE WHAT WAKES ME. Through my cabin window I can see that it is just dawn, still Mom's watch. Weather must be changing; a thin line of red indicates the rising sun. Mom has throttled up the engine, and the sound rattles the inside of the boat. Duncan won't be happy about her revving the engine. I close my eyes. Then, over the din of the engine, I hear my mother's voice on the two-way VHF radio at the chart table. She must be using the handheld radio in the cockpit.

"Mayday, mayday, mayday."

My feet find the cold floor of my cabin. I toss on my sailing jacket over my pajamas and bolt from the cabin.

Duncan's door is still closed, and I bang on it as I scramble up the companionway steps.

There's a thudding crunch on one side of the hull that almost shakes me off the steps. Then another. Duncan's door crashes open and he emerges, his hair all rucked up and his eyes still doped with sleep. I can hear another boat engine. Duncan pushes past me on the steps.

Over his head I see a flare streak low. Mom's fired a distress flare. She's screaming for Duncan.

"Get below!" Duncan shoves me down the steps.

I follow him back up. At the top of the steps he stops, and I peer out into the cockpit from under his elbow. I can see a dhow, an open wooden boat motoring alongside, thudding into our hull. The three men in the boat are shouting at my mother. Ski masks cover their faces. From the edge of the sun, another boat hurtles toward us.

I sense the gunfire more than hear it. It's like the sound is inside my head, and I swear I can feel my eardrums vibrate as if they are making the sound. I duck my head lower into the companionway. Duncan is yelling at Mom, "Those are warning shots. Cut the engine. They won't hurt us if we cooperate."

I push up onto the last step so I'm standing beside Duncan. Mom's eyes are crazed with fear. Maybe she doesn't hear him over the sound of the engines. Maybe she's hearing Jimmy's voice in her head. She levels a flare right at the oncoming boat. I lose her for a moment in the smoke of the flare. The flare rockets toward the boat and explodes on their bow.

I know why moviemakers sometimes film action sequences in slow motion. It's because that's the way we see it in real life. It's like a strobe light catches the horror in flashes so that the images can burn into our brains. So that we can't hope to ever forget it.

The second boat is so much closer now that I can see the gunman. He too is wearing a ski mask, as are the other men in his boat. He's standing at the bow of his boat, a large rifle aimed our way. His whole body shakes with the force of the weapon. Tiny bursts of fire erupt from the barrel followed by the blat-blat-blat sound of automatic gunfire.

A spray rips across the mainsail. A cockpit cushion explodes in shards of foam. Then the Thermos of tea disintegrates. Maybe I imagine it, but I think I see tea droplets hang in the air. The noise is enormous but even so, I can hear Duncan, beside me, screaming at my mother. I think he's telling her to drop. He's scrambling out into the cockpit, running toward my mother. But nothing is faster than the bullets. Not his words. Not me thinking, *Oh good, they're going to miss her.*

They don't. With the impact of the bullets, my mother spins, her arms splayed back in an almost graceful arch. Red goo shoots from one pant leg. I see the soles of her boots, and then she crashes facedown onto the floor of the cockpit.

In one agonizing sound Duncan calls for my mother and cries out as the bullets catch him in midair and his left shoulder shatters. He rolls with the impact, flying now, his feet no longer in contact with the boat. More gunfire, and his skull lifts away like a red and gray cap. I close my eyes and when I open them, he's gone, clear over the side of the boat. Then the gunfire stops.

The first boat accelerates toward our bow. As it passes I see the men gathering what looks like a fishing net from the bottom of their boat. Mustn't run into a fishing net. Fishing nets will foul your propeller and stop you dead. I can't see them throw the net in front of our boat, but with a strangling sound, our engine dies. In the sudden silence, I'm aware that I'm screaming. The second boat comes to a shuddering stop against our hull. The first boat pulls up against our transom and men from both boats board *Mistaya*.

My legs give out and I crumple onto the top step of the companionway. I can see Mom lifting her head, struggling with the radio. The man with the gun steps over her, glances at me, then he shouts in anger. He cracks the butt of the gun into the back of my mother's head. She looks up, then her eyes roll back and her head drops limply onto the cockpit floor. The screams stop in my throat.

Waving the gun, the gunman motions two of the men to our cabin roof. Pulling large knives out of their belts, the men leap onto the cockpit seats, their legs just inches away from my face. Grunting, they lower our rolled-up inflatable dinghy off the cabin roof into one of their boats. Other men proceed to strip the outside of our boat.

I clamp my hand over my mouth, willing myself to be quiet. The men are shouting at each other. All of them have knives. Two of them burst down the companionway stairs, one pushing me out of his way, the other shoving me ahead of him down into the boat. The gunman follows. With his elbow he knocks me against the cabin wall. I can practically feel the cold of the gun so close to my face. One man seems to check the sleeping cabins, says something to the gunman, and the gunman nods. Abruptly, he turns his back on me. At the chart table the gunman rips open drawers. In one he finds a wallet, Duncan's wallet. Duncan said once that if you make some things easy to find, then maybe a thief would be happy with that and leave. The gunman thumbs through the wallet and pockets the cash, then he shakes it in my face, shouting. The wallet doesn't seem to be enough.

The other two men cut the wires to the electronics and rip out our radio and navigation equipment. Then they start tearing open lockers. One opens the fridge, grabs one of the plastic food containers and peels back the lid. His lip curls, but he scoops his dirty fingers into the cold lasagna and eats it. Then he throws the container across the cabin, spewing lasagna trails.

I can feel my heart thudding through my jacket. I press my back against the cabin wall, trying to disappear into the wood grain.

Five men are packed into the boat so close I can smell them. They're wearing long-sleeved shirts and work pants. Some are barefoot; some are wearing cheap rubber flip-flops I recognize from the bazaars of Djibouti. But bazaars everywhere sell cheap rubber flip-flops. All I can see of the men is their eyes and mouths and their hands. Some are dark. All are the lined hands of working men. All are dirty.

One lifts the floorboards of the boat and hoots when he finds Duncan's stash of booze. He lobs a bottle of single-malt scotch to the gunman and opens another for himself. He pours the alcohol down his throat, then smears his mouth with the back of his hand.

The man at the fridge finds the eggs. Laughing, he strews the carton so that a dozen eggs are missiles in the cabin. An egg explodes on the wall beside me and the broken shell peppers my cheek. My hands are useless to wipe it away, my limbs useless to even move, like everything in me is liquid. The egg slime splatters, then slumps down the wall.

Now the men from outside jam themselves below, jostling for the booze bottles as they rip apart our sleeping cabins. I hear drawers being yanked out and dumped on the floor. In my cabin, they must be shoveling my school texts off the shelf because loose-leaf paper sails across the cabin. In front of me, one of the men uses his knife to slit open my pillow, then tosses it back into my cabin.

The gunman is screaming at one of the men who seems to be admiring a Timex watch he took from my cabin. The gunman strikes the man's hand and the watch flies to the floor. The egg man finds this funny. The gunman crushes the watch with his heel.

In Duncan and my mother's cabin a bottle breaks, and the smell of my mother's perfume fills the boat. It's not the scent of my mother that I would smell when I used to hug her, the skin and powder and perfume scent of her shoulders. It's an explosion of smell, and I hold my breath against it.

Now some of the men go out to the cockpit and the ones inside throw them the stuff they've torn from our boat. They take everything: gear, clothing, cans of food, all the booze, binoculars and electronics and gauges. They empty Duncan's locker of spare engine parts. They take Duncan's tools. They take my shampoo.

On the floor, the heaps of books hurled from the shelves come up past my ankles. Glass from a shattered jar of raspberry jam is scattered in red sticky bits all over the cabin. A bag of rice, slit open, disgorges pearl pellets under my feet. Locker doors are torn off. Severed wiring looks like plastic spaghetti. Cushions have been sliced and stuffing yanked out. Long gouges on the dining table make me think of claw marks.

One of the wooden boats' engines starts, and I feel our boat rock as some of the men jump down into their boat. Their engine revs up. I hear their boat scrape against ours, then their engine roar as they take off.

I'm aware that my hands are slippery with sweat. Sweat runs down my back. The remaining men toe the refuse on the floor of the cabin, sifting through the heaps for anything they might have missed. The gunman drains his bottle of whiskey. Behind the mask, his eyes are rimmed with red. He's looking at me, then he screams at me, his mouth so close that his spit sprays my face. The other men look at him, then at me. I have no idea what he's saying. He grabs me and shoves me toward the steps to the cockpit. When the gunman grabs my arm, his hand goes right round it. Still shouting, the gunman pushes me up the steps.

My mother is motionless on the floor of the cockpit. Her hood covers her face. Blood is trickling from her leg, and I'm happy because that means her heart is beating, that she's alive. But there is a lot of blood. I step toward her, but the gunman jerks me back.

The cockpit and deck feel strangely bare. Anything of value has been taken. Even the box of flares is gone. The wind has come up and the mainsail is flapping, the wind whistling through the bullet holes. The gunman looks up at the sky. Black clouds form an inverted bowl overhead. The gunman hollers something at the men in the cabin, and they too climb up into the cockpit. Their arms are loaded with huge bundles of our stuff, which they toss down to their waiting boat. The building waves knock their boat against ours.

I don't want to be out here. Somehow I feel safer in the stink and mess below. One of the men nudges me, the one who had such a good time with the eggs. I don't know if he meant to touch me. I recoil from him, which makes him laugh. The man pokes me in the ribs, intentionally now. I bat away his hand. All the men laugh. He reeks of booze. He leans in close to me, Eggman, so close that all I have to breathe is his stink of booze and my mother's lasagna. For an endless moment he hangs in front of my face. Then he kisses me.

It's not so much a kiss as a crushing of lips and teeth and tongue, God, a thick, prodding mass of tongue that fills my mouth. I gag and twist my face away. Eggman grabs my chin with greasy fingers, his thumb digging deeply into the underside of my chin so that I can't breathe. His saliva is drying on my lips and I want to wipe it off. But I leave my arms at my sides. I will myself to a blank place of not knowing, not knowing that my mother is laying at my feet in a puddle of blood, that Duncan is blown apart on the sea, that it's only me with these men.

I think about a starving cat I saw in Djibouti, bones hard through its skin, and the expressionless way it gulped the bread I gave it, like it didn't care if I killed it, that maybe death was looking pretty good. At least for Duncan, it was quick.

Eggman licks his lips. I close my eyes. If I try, if I really focus, I can hear my own heart beating, the blood pulsing through the tiniest vessels into the deepest places of my brain. If I try, then I don't have to know what Eggman is doing.

Lightning bursts over the boat, so close that the light and sound erupt in the same instant. A gust hits the boat like a hammer and the deck slopes crazily. Eggman drops his hand as he struggles for footing, stumbling to his knees. I fall away from him. Even in the lee of our sailboat, waves slop over the sides of their boat. The gunman screams at the men.

At first I think the sound is the gun, a tremendous tearing noise that makes me duck my head. The gunman glances up, and I see the mainsail, peppered with bullet holes, shred in the wind. It's crazy, but I almost feel like laughing. The mainsail is in rags, snapping at the mast. Even without the sail, the wind is heeling us over so that the men have to hang on to stand up. I'm in the cockpit of the only world I have, in the middle of some sea half a planet away from the only world I know. I'm with a killer and his thugs. And the storm has moved right on top of our heads.

Maybe I do laugh.

The gunman slings his gun across his back. He kicks Eggman in the ass and Eggman lurches to his feet. The second man says something. They all laugh. I see Eggman's hand come up, fast, and I can't move, probably wouldn't have moved even if I could. His fist crashes into the side of my face. White heat explodes in my jaw, in my sinus, in my temple, and my knees fold. The last thing I see is our red go-bag being tossed down into their boat.

SIX

I DON'T WANT TO OPEN my eyes. I've ignored the slamming of the boat, the crunching sound my shoulders make as I launch into one cockpit bench, then the other. It's the waves breaking over the boat that make me attempt to move, to escape the icy green water. Each new wave flattens me to the cockpit floor.

I raise my head and open my eyes. The sky has collapsed to black, the sun indiscernible. I can't tell how long I've been laying here, but I've lost all feeling in my hands and feet. The wind shrieks through the rigging, flogging the remains of the mainsail as if it were a manic bass guitar. Beyond the stern, the sea is endless waves, seamless gray with the sky. Wind rips the tops from the waves in white flumes, flings the sea in horizontal blades against my face. Wind twists my hair to wire and snaps it across my cheeks and mouth.

Farther back in the cockpit, crumpled against the wheel post, my mother is a tumble of yellow.

"Mom." I take a breath, then another, and struggle to my knees. Black dots dance in front of my eyes. I force myself to breathe. The dots clear. Pain knuckles me at the base of my skull, then radiates over my entire head. More black dots. Then I take a wave full in the face. I duck another wave so that it hits me in the back. My jacket hangs heavy, dripping water. My pajamas cling like wet tissue on my legs.

I'm aware that I'm not tethered, that a rogue wave could wash me right through the open transom. The waves pitch the boat in a drunken roll that drives my hip and shoulder against the cockpit with a crack. Scrabbling from one hand-hold to the next, I pull myself to my mother.

Her eyes are closed. Her lips are lined in blue. Behind her, the sea gapes great open jaws. "Mom?" I put one hand on her face. She's cold, like the storm water, like my hands. Frantic, I set my cheek against her mouth. I feel a small warmth. The storm steals each tiny exhalation, but she's breathing.

When I was really young, if I woke up in the night, I'd stand beside my mother's bed, watching her sleep, waiting for her to wake. Even asleep, my mother's face was animate. Now, she doesn't look asleep. It looks like she's dead.

"I need to get you down below, out of the storm." I unclip her tether, holding on to her by the hood of her jacket. As the seas lift the stern of the boat, I cross my mother's arms over her chest and yank her by her elbows toward the companionway. Her VHF radio still hangs on her wrist, and as I pull her it bangs on the floor of the cockpit. I'm aware of a slick of red that trails one boot, but I'm not looking at my mother's leg. Not yet. Now I just want to get us below, away from the waves.

I struggle to reach the handholds at the companionway. I'll have to ease my mother down first. As the boat rolls into the trough of the waves, I fold her onto the steps, then, grasping her tether to slow her fall, I let her slither to the cabin floor. A wave follows her down the companionway.

Over my shoulder, I look to the back of the boat. Duncan can't still be there. That's why we wear a tether, so that if we go overboard, we stay with the boat. He didn't have a tether; he won't be there.

I have to be sure. Still on my hands and knees, and pulling myself with my hands, I inch my way to the back of the boat. Seawater pierces my eyes and I blink. For a second, I think I see him, his white head bobbing on the waves, but it's just foam from the waves. In every direction, all I see is the storm. I know he's gone. I just hope he died before he hit the water.

My feet are slippery on the companionway steps as I scramble down to my mother.

HANGING ON WITH one hand, I reach up to haul closed the hatch. Now the screaming wind doesn't steal my breath and drill into my ears. I make my way down into the boat.

With every step the floor pitches and disappears under my feet. It's louder being inside the boat, like being inside a drum. The wind resonates in the mast, boom and rigging so that the hull vibrates with the howl of it, magnifying it. Open locker doors slam back and forth against the bulkheads. A set of enamelled plates behind one locker door lift and clatter like cymbals. Curtains at the windows sway out to vertical, then drop back against the acrylic panes. A juice glass rockets from one open locker and shatters on the opposite wall.

Everything on the floor now swims in half a foot of seawater. I latch down a couple of floating floorboards so that I won't step into the bilge.

Swinging by one arm, I fish the top boards of the dining bench out of our slough and replace them. The bench cushion is hopelessly sodden and I leave it on the floor. "Looks like you'll have to sleep on the hard plywood." Pulling myself hand over hand against the rolling of the boat, I find a quilt that is reasonably dry. "I'll fold this up for you." I position the quilt along the dining bench, then fit the canvas lee cloths that will hold Mom in like a hammock. Mom calls the dining bench a sea berth and sleeps here when we're at sea. She says it's the best bed in the boat because it rocks less, like being on the middle of a teeter-totter versus the ends. In a storm like this, it's a subtle distinction.

I think of Fanny's basket hammock, of Emma and Mac's snug boat. They wouldn't have heard my mother's mayday. We're just too far away. I was too late getting back to the boat. My throat closes and my eyes fill, and I push the thought out of my mind.

In all her gear my mother weighs a ton, and I can only use one arm to lift her because I have to hold on with the other. I hoist half of her onto the bench, then, anchoring her chest with my knee, I strip off her jacket. Underneath, her fleece is wet around the neck so I take this off, and her sweatshirt. Her final layer, a T-shirt, is reasonably dry and I leave it. Now for the pants. The one pant leg hangs in yellow ribbons. Gripping the waist band, I ease Mom's pants down to her boots. The inner layers are sodden with blood. Taking a breath, I peel back what's left of the fabric.

From the middle of her thigh, a thin river of red runs into my mother's boot.

The breath stops in my chest. I grab her sweatshirt and wad it against her leg, wrapping the sleeves of the shirt around. If I had another set of hands, if I even had both of mine, I'd do all that direct pressure stuff you learn in first aid. I can barely tie a knot in the sleeves of the sweatshirt.

I lower Mom's head to the quilt. "You'll be fine." My voice is shaking, my hands too. I take off one boot, the good one. Seawater dumps into the cabin. The other boot spills red onto my pajamas.

I push Mom onto her side and draw the quilt around her. The sweatshirt seems to be stemming the worst of the bleeding. I tighten the lee cloths. She's cocooned now, just her pale face visible outside of the lee cloths. I slump down on the bench beside her. My jaw hurts where I got slugged. Every joint in my body feels like someone has driven nails into it.

I take my mother's jacket and untangle the radio. The battery light shows a pale yellow. "Not much battery left."

I glance around the mess that is our cabin. "Maybe I can recharge it if I can find the charging unit."

Looking around, I see Eggman left the fridge open. I reach over and drop the lid, then switch off the breakers on the main electrical panel. The fridge motor falls silent.

"But right now everyone is in their own private storm. And they're so far away they won't hear us anyway." I'm cold suddenly, so cold my hands shake and my teeth chatter. I need dry clothes. I set the radio in its spot at the chart table and, hanging on for every step, I slog through seawater to my cabin. It's like being drunk, this feeling, an overwhelming need to lay down. There is less water in my cabin. I rip off my wet clothes, leaving them in a puddle on the floor, hang my jacket on a hook and ransack a pile of clothes to find a T-shirt and shorts. My hands fumble as I put on the clothes. So cold. I jam my mattress back into place and turn over my slashed pillow, then crawl into the bunk. My quilt is gone, but I find a blanket that is dry and wrap it around me. My knees are weak, everything is weak, my head feels too heavy for my neck. Using the pillow as a brace against the storm, I cram myself into a ball in the corner of my bunk. I cover my ears to block out the howling wind. I don't close my eyes because when I do, I see Eggman, and Duncan, so I lie there and listen to the blood racing through my arteries and veins and capillaries, and wish I could stop shaking.

SEVEN

FOR ONE LONG MINUTE, I think I've gone blind. Then I realize that I've fallen asleep, and now it's dark. I have no idea if it's just night, or almost morning. All I know is I must have been sleeping for hours.

"Mom!" How could I just leave her like that? What if she woke up and thought she was alone?

"I'm coming, Mom." Automatically I reach for the flashlight clamped on the wall by my bed. It's not there, of course. I wrestle out of the bunk and swing my feet to the floor. The shock of cold water past my ankles makes me gasp. We're taking on water, a lot of water. Not good. I try to swallow the panic rising in my gut and wade out to the main cabin.

I still have to hang on, but the motion in the boat now feels like angry aftershocks. The books and debris on the floor have transformed into a kind of pulp porridge. I feel my way to the dining table.

"Mom?" I can't see her, not in the dark, but I find her face with my hand. "Are you awake?"

Under my hand, she stirs, moans, then falls quiet again. "Mom?"

No response. Her skin feels warmer. I listen to her breathing, matching my intake with hers, grateful for every breath. "I didn't mean to fall asleep. I was just so cold." I tug the quilt tighter over her shoulders and make sure her feet are covered. "You're okay. You're going to be fine." Right.

I slog my way to the locker where we keep our boots. In the dark I can't tell if the boots are mine or Duncan's, not that it matters. I pour the water out of the boots, then put them on. Now I don't have to worry about slicing my feet open on broken glass. The breaker panel is dark. When I flipped all the breakers, I turned off the bilge pump too. I wonder how much battery juice a bilge pump needs to expel a small swimming pool from the inside of a boat? What I do know is that a bilge pump can't handle sodden textbooks. With my boot, I stir the mess in the water. "I've got to get rid of this stuff."

It's probably just as well that I can't see what I'm doing. Using the plastic garbage pail, I sift the bilge water for armfuls of debris that I dump in the bucket. Then I haul the bucket up the steps to the cockpit, and dump it into the cockpit. The cockpit is designed to drain itself, and the stuff I pour in flows out over the stern through the open transom. Big stuff, like cushions, I just heave out into the cockpit, not caring if they blow overboard. I am a one-woman environmental disaster. Out goes one of the plastic food containers. Another I find seems to be still closed, and I taste the contents. Lasagna. The cold congealed pasta makes my stomach roll and I can't choke it down. I remember when my mother was making the lasagna the day before we set out. She'd been thrilled to find the right kind of cheese at the market, not Mozzarella, but something that would work. Small victories gave her such pleasure. Then I think about Eggman, and I toss the container out into the cockpit.

I find what feels like Duncan's chart and stretch it out to dry on the chart table. I find a Tetra Pak and open it, hoping it might be juice. It's milk, but I drink from it, then set the container in the sink to finish later. I find a flashlight, but the water has ruined it. I find buckets and buckets of broken glass and soggy rice. Everything goes overboard. When pale dawn lightens the gray sky in the east, I'm sieving the water for anything that might clog the pump when I turn it on. My arms and shoulders are sore, my knuckles are bleeding from scraping against the floor. The wind has eased, but the sea is still churning. Sometimes it takes days for the sea to settle after a storm. It's like the sea won't let go of the fury.

I flop down on the dining bench beside Mom. I pull up my knees to my chest and look at her. Her eyebrows are twitching and her eyes are moving under her lids as if she's dreaming. I reach over and run my fingers over her cheeks.

She starts and her eyes open.

I shout, I can't help it, "Mom!"

She flinches from the sound.

I'm so happy to see her that I laugh. "You're awake!"

Her eyes find mine. She struggles to focus. She says something, but her voice is barely a croak.

"You need a drink." But in the time it takes to grab a water bottle from the table her eyes are closed again.

"Mom!"

Her mouth moves, a smile or a grimace, I can't tell, then she slips again into sleep.

I say a very bad word. Then I give her a shake. "Don't you leave me like this!"

Her eyelids barely flutter.

Dread crawls over me. I throw the quilt off of her and peel away the sweatshirt. It's heavy with blood and I throw it out of the boat. Her leg has stopped bleeding and I see now that there are two bullet holes, fairly small, one on the front of her thigh toward the side, the other a little lower and behind. Gently, I prod the wounds. Mom moans, but her eyes stay closed. If she's lucky, the two wounds means that she was hit with one bullet, that it went in and out. I run my hand over the long leg bone of her thigh. I don't know what broken bone feels like, but Mom's leg feels about like it should. Maybe the bullet missed the bone.

The first aid kit in the galley has been ripped open and scattered. On the counter I find a package of sterile dressings. I take out a couple, grab a cloth and a bowl of water and go back to Mom.

The bullet holes are crusted with blood, and I clean around the wounds, careful not to make them bleed again. A thin clear ooze runs from the wound on the front of her leg. I wipe it away as best as I can. She's not bleeding anymore, that's good. I don't know how much blood she lost, maybe a lot. Maybe too much. I push that thought from my mind and cover the bullet wounds with the dressing.

On the back of her head the gunman left Mom a bump the size of an orange. But it's just a bump, right? Everyone gets bumps on their head. It doesn't mean she has a concussion. If she did have a concussion, what are you supposed to do? I seem to remember something about waking them up every few hours, that they sleep like the dead. No. Not like the dead. I give Mom another shake. She mutters but doesn't stir. I also remember she needs to be on her side with her chin tilted, so that her tongue doesn't fall back and close off her air passage. And it's not good for someone to rest in the same position for too long, so I roll her onto her other side. That gets more of a reaction. Mom's eyes bug wide and she gasps. But then she sighs, like she's tired, and closes her eyes again.

I'm tired too. I flip the quilt over her and tuck it in around her legs. In a way, I'm glad she doesn't know how much shit we're in.

I get up and fill the garbage pail with water. "Okay. I know. There's still too much water. I'll use all our battery power just draining the water. And no power is no good." I grunt as I hurl the water out into the cockpit where it drains away. "So I'll bail." I fill another pail. And another. The work mesmerizes me. The pain in my arms and shoulders gives me something to bite into. Pail after pail after pail of water goes overboard. I stop to rest and I hear it.

Something is bumping against the hull. Thump. Bump. Bump. Thump. Bump. Bump.

I bail. It erases the noise. But when I can no longer hoist the pail, then I stop. And I hear it.

"You know what that is, don't you?" I go over and nudge my mother. *"Don't You?"*

I cover my ears, but I feel it if I don't hear it. Thump. Bump. Bump.

I clear the companionway in two steps. *"I know it's you!"* I scream at the sea behind the boat. *"You're dead. D. E. A. D. Leave me alone!"*

Thump. Bump. Bump.

I lean over the stern rail. *"Don't do this to me."* In the rising sun, the sea is grayish green, the breaking waves are gone, leaving behind deep smooth troughs between ten-foot swells. His shape is yellow, a watery yellow in the green of the sea, just below the surface. His hood hangs forward, the arms waft out to the side. But Duncan wasn't wearing his yellow jacket, so it can't be Duncan. I must have thrown his jacket overboard. Other stuff I've tossed overboard lingers in the waves. There's the lasagna container, bobbing empty now, and a tin in which we keep saltines. The empty yellow jacket sleeves undulate. They motion to me. The reflective tape on the jacket flashes in the new sun.

Thump. Bump. Bump.

"You're free now." I wave my arms at the jacket. "Ashes to ashes." With a suddenness that makes me gasp, the yellow of the jacket disappears below the surface. "Duncan!" I search the water and maybe there is one final small flash of light, but maybe I just want it so I see it. He was never there. Duncan was never, ever, there.

EIGHT

"IF YOU THINK," I HURL a bucket of water out of the cabin into the cockpit where it drains away, "that this changes anything," I refill the bucket, "then you're crazy." My arms are burning with the effort of hoisting bucket after bucket of water. "I have enough to do, thank you very much."

I know she can't hear me. Even if she could, what's she going to do? Jump out of her bed and rescue us? Still, I talk to her. It fills the emptiness. "Yes, we have the radio. But the radio battery is low. Low, low, low." My pail scrapes against the floor as I bail. I've got almost all of the water out of the boat. "And who knows where the charging unit is. Maybe one of the pirates is putting it on his mantle right now, like a trophy." I hoist the bucket out. "We have to get closer to our friends, closer to anyone, before we call for help." No one is hearing us where we are. No one except the pirates. I quickly squelch that image. "So if you just want to lay there, fine. But don't expect me to keep you company. It's that simple."

I remove the last of the water with a mop. At least I can see the floor again. The boat still looks like hell. I've managed to cram everything back into place, but it reminds me of cleaning up the house after a party when nothing looks quite like it did before. I found an opened package of cookies that escaped the water, and I take these and the milk carton and sit on the bench beside my mother.

"Yum. Hobnobs. You love these cookies." I break a bit of the cookie into my mouth. The buttery sweetness makes my mouth water. Even the milk tastes good, and normally I hate Tetra Pak milk. UHT, ugly horrible taste, but it lasts forever. I eat the cookie, then pry another from the pack. "I'll try to save some for you."

I lean back so that I can see her face. The cookie snaps in my fingers and the milk stops in my throat. Mom's eyes are wide open.

I swear, then say, "You startled me!" Her eyes swivel up to mine. "You're awake. That's very good." I try to smile, but the ghostly color in her face makes it difficult. She doesn't speak and her eyes seem fixed and glazed.

"Mom?"

No response.

I grab a water bottle and hold it to her lips. "You must be thirsty. Have some water." I squirt a small stream into her mouth.

Her eyes widen and she coughs, weakly at first, then she sucks a breath and coughs again. Her eyes fill; she draws one more interminably long breath, then finally clears the water from her throat.

"I'm sorry. I'm so sorry. I gave you too much." I hold the water bottle against her lips. "I'll be more careful." This time I dribble the water over her tongue and she swallows it. I hold my breath. Her forehead crinkles as if in pain, but she drinks slowly, fighting for every swallow, and she drinks the bottle down. Then her eyes close again.

"Mom?" I sweep the hair from her forehead. Louder this time, "Mom!" I press my hand against her forehead, willing her to open her eyes. Her head feels heavy, inert. She's out again.

My throat clenches and tears hit me so that I'm sobbing like a little kid. *"Mom!"* I want to crawl into the berth with her like I used to do a million years ago when I'd get into bed with her in the night and she'd put her arm around me and pull me against her, vanquishing whatever had sent me running in the dark.

I wipe my eyes on my shirt, sniff my nose. This is like every Disney movie, with the mother or father always getting offed, leaving the young on their own to face the perils of the wilderness or the wicked witch or whatever. Of course they're never all alone. Cinderella had the fairy godmother; Simba had the farting warthog. I'd take a farting warthog right now, anything other than this being alone.

I climb out into the cockpit. The sun is directly over my head. Noon. There's no wind, although the waves wrench the boom back and forth over the cockpit. The pirates used a fishing net to foul our propeller. I know something about this because once, before we left Australia, Duncan backed down on a dock line that I'd left trailing in the water. It took Duncan over an hour in the water, diving down to the propeller, hacking away the rope, coming back up for a gulp of air, before he could start the engine again. In Australia, the water was so clear you could see the bottom. It was just one rope, not an entire net. Now, we're in the middle of the Red Sea. Goose bumps lift up on my arms.

There is nothing left of the mainsail, but I could unfurl the headsail, maybe, except that there's no wind.

"What do you expect of me, anyway?" I slam my fist against the side of the boat. "I'm fourteen. I can still fit into clothes from the kids' department." My throat aches with fatigue and new tears threaten. "I could quit right now and no one would blame me. Not Dad, that's for sure." Dad can get lost in a parkade. Dad says we're heroes for going on this trip. Especially me, he says, because I'm normal, not an adventure-crazed thrill-seeker. I'm not sure that Mom or Duncan fit that description either, but they definitely have more adventures than Dad. When we were together, Dad's idea of a high-risk experience was staying at a two-star hotel. The first thing Mom did after the divorce was take me camping in Mexico to see the pyramids. Dad made me pack water-purification tablets, not that he needed to worry. Mom wouldn't let me even rinse my toothbrush with tap water.

I wonder what he's doing now, Dad? It's the middle of the night where he is.

I don't even know which rope is for the headsail. I study the jumble of multicolored ropes in the cockpit. "So much for neat-and-tidy, Duncan. I guess the storm undid your coils." Each rope feeds through a cleat on the cabin roof. Each of these is labeled, of course. I find the cleat labeled *Mainsheet* and haul on that rope to secure the boom. The one marked *Headsail/Genoa* I begin to unravel from the others.

When Duncan unfurled the genoa, he did it at the same time as he pulled it in on one side of the boat or the other. That way the sail doesn't flail, which I guess is hard on the sailcloth. I know which ropes control the sail. ("Sheets, Lib, not ropes." I get it, Duncan.) These feed through blocks on either side of the cockpit and have figure-eight knots in the ends. This was the first knot I learned to tie, the figure-eight stopper knot. Duncan taught me using a string of black licorice. Every knot I tied right I could bite off and eat. My mother hates black licorice. Duncan's not wild about it either. He bought it because I like it.

In the mess of ropes I find one sodden flare that disintegrates when I pick it up. I toss the ruined flare in the sea. I coil all the ropes, making sense of which go where, including the one attached to the top of the mainsail. This one is called a halyard, who knows why. If I lowered the mainsail, I could pack the rags of sail into the long canvas bag attached to the boom. The pirates took Duncan's spare sails, so there's nothing to hoist in place of the tattered mainsail, but at least the useless sail would be out of the way and not making me crazy with the flapping. I've never done this job by myself either, but I've helped Duncan and my mother. They like to lower the sail into orderly folds that they flake evenly over the boom before drawing the bag around it. I'm not after beautiful sail stowage. I uncleat the halyard and let the rope fly.

About half the sail plummets into the cockpit, an immense expanse of tattered sailcloth that piles onto my head. Cursing, I mound it onto the boom and cram it down inside the canvas bag. The boom is higher than I'm tall, so I stuff the sail above my head, feeling with my hands where there's room to shove more sail. With each armful of sail-cloth I'm able to stow, more bursts free from the constraints of the bag. Finally, though, I can pull the rest of the sail down into the bag. As lumpy as I've stuffed the bag, it's impossible to pull the zipper closed to hold everything in place. Instead, I wrap the boom in three places with webbing straps. The bag looks like a giant snake that's eaten several distinct meals.

I turn my attention to the headsail. Furled, the genoa is wound into a tight roll at the bow of the boat. In a perfect world, it will unwind into a powerful, pulling wing. But it is not a perfect world, that much I know. I let slip the furling line.

There's not much wind, so the genoa uncoils like a flaccid flag. Optimistically, I winch it in on the left side of the boat, cleating the genoa sheet, ready for the imaginary wind that will take me out of here.

Although, which way I should steer is not immediately clear. The gunman's bullets managed to miss the compass on the steering post. I remember from plotting the course with Emma that we're heading northwest, not that I'm going anywhere anyway. I flop down onto the cockpit bench. Shielding my eyes from the sun, I tip my head to rest on the back of the bench.

Each one of my muscles feels like an over-stretched rubber band. There must be several hundred muscles just in the back of my neck. The ones in my legs are denying all direction from my brain. Apparently, I even have muscles in my lungs, because the act of breathing is difficult.

The others in the flotilla will be wringing themselves out after the storm. Emma has her foul weather gear hung out to dry in the cockpit. Mac is making them lunch, a peppery omelet, maybe.

The thought of the eggs broken below, and Eggman, makes the milk in my stomach turn over.

They won't even know that we left port. They probably think we got an updated weather forecast and we were the smart ones to stay put, that we were snug on the seawall, fighting over whether "xerox" is a permissible Scrabble word, while they were fighting to keep their masts out of the sea.

As I sit here, Jimmy's wife is making BLTs with tomatoes from Djibouti, each tomato costing more than some workers make in a month, and Jimmy cleans the barrel of his

M–16, eyeing the horizon for the happy chance to unload it into someone.

I wouldn't mind if Jimmy chose Eggman and his boss. I really wouldn't.

We never should have left. We should have waited for the next flotilla. We'd never catch up with Emma and Mac, never see them again, but somehow I don't think we're going to anyway.

I never should have left my mother alone in the cockpit.

If I could use the engine, I could travel in the general direction of the flotilla. Not that I'd ever find them, even. I might be able to find a commercial ship, but if you believe Jimmy, they wouldn't respond to a radio call. Not that I can use the engine, not with the fish net wrapped around the propeller. Not that I'm going anywhere.

Not that Duncan or my mother can help me. This morning, my mother's sweatshirt smelled sour with blood. The smell reminded me of a meat shop we once went into, dim, with sawdust on the floor and the skinned carcasses of goats and sheep suspended from a low ceiling. My mother asked for lamb, and the butcher unhooked a small carcass and tossed it onto a wooden chopping block in the middle of his shop. With an immense knife he pried free a rack of ribs, rehung the rest of the lamb, then, with a cleaver, whacked the ribs into chops. Duncan told me to stand back, but I didn't, and bits of bone and blood hit my cheek.

With that image, the cookies and milk rise up in my throat, abate, then with a burning fierceness, burst out my mouth and nostrils, spraying the cockpit floor. I cough, heave what's left and heave again. I haven't thrown up since second grade and I've forgotten how vomit scalds the nasal passages. I'm crying again, my nose running all down my face. I bring my feet up out of the mess, onto the bench, bending my knees under my chin. My hands smell of vomit. I want someone to come and clean me up. I want someone to deal with the toss. Tossed cookies, literally. The movement of the boat is sloshing the puddle back and forth on the floor of the cockpit.

I grab the bucket Mom keeps tied to the stern rail, drop it over the side to fill it, haul it in, and slosh the cockpit mess out over the transom. Bending over the rail to refill the bucket, I stop myself from looking at the sea, at the inevitable panic I feel at the thought of falling in.

With the mess finally gone, I collapse onto the cockpit bench. Next time I'll just hurl into the bucket. That's what Mom does. On passage, the green bucket is her best friend. She carries it with her like a handbag.

Duncan says, or Duncan said, I mean, that fear can make a person seasick. I don't think of my mother as a fearful person. Cautious, for sure, and a bit manic when it comes to germs, worms and things you can catch from doorknobs. I remember once when I was really little grossing her out in a public washroom by crawling on my hands and knees under the cubicle doors. Apparently, and I know this because when I emerged from my commando crawl, she drilled it into my head for the full five minutes that she scoured my hands: The highest concentration of germs in a bathroom is not on the toilet seat, or even the bowl, but on the floor. I have no idea how this can be, but I still wouldn't test the theory by touching a toilet seat in a public washroom.

Ty, once, at McDonald's, followed me into the women's restroom. It made me laugh the way he just walked in like it was perfectly normal and acceptable. I don't think anyone even noticed, and if they did, Ty wouldn't have cared. In the tiny stall, I wondered if I'd ever get the knees of my jeans clean and if people would be able to tell from my jeans what I'd done.

Duncan says, or said, that what doesn't kill you makes you strong.

I reach for the bucket again.

NINE

THE ONSET OF NIGHT MAKES me anxious. I'm not afraid of the dark, but it's unnerving, not being able to see. I'll find myself constantly reaching for a light switch. Since mid-afternoon, Mom has been making noises in her sleep, little moans that have increased in volume. She's woken a few times, and I was able to give her a little water. I had to change her quilt. When I unwrapped her to check her leg wounds, I found that she'd peed herself. I managed to get a pair of shorts on her and improvised a diaper with sanitary pads. This should test how much these things really hold. Mom's gunshot wounds look about the same except now there's more weeping fluid. I washed the wounds and covered them with clean dressings. Then with fresh water I washed her, head to toe, and brushed the snarls out of her hair. Afterward I turned her in her berth and wrapped a dry quilt around her. She cried out when I turned her and woke long enough to drink some. She feels a little warm, but I might be imagining that.

I washed the soiled quilt in a bucket of seawater. It was bloody and could have used a proper hot wash and laundry soap cleaning, but that's a luxury for port. We've spent entire days in port doing laundry. I wrung out the quilt, then rinsed it in a bit of fresh water so that it would dry soft, and hung it over the boom to dry. The air probably did as much to freshen the quilt as the washing.

I don't feel like eating anything, but I open a pouch of tuna. It's strange what the pirates took, like the canned corned beef, the stuff with a cow head on the label. I can't stand it, none of us liked it, that's why we still had several tins of it in the locker. Mom bought a crate of it in Australia because she said all sailors eat canned corned beef. The pirates took every last one, loading it into a pillowcase like it was Halloween. And the sardines in mustard sauce, they're welcome to those. A lot of the labels have come off the cans, either from floating in bilge water or sometimes Mom takes off the labels if she's afraid there might be cockroach eggs under them. Then she writes the contents on the lid of the can. I eat the tuna straight from the package, then drink the milk I had opened earlier. The milk is warm so I plug my nose and chug it; I won't have to taste it.

With darkness settling into the corners of the boat, I make a final check of my mother—her moaning has subsided—and the boat. Out in the cockpit, I see the headsail tugging on the sheet, just fretting with it, nothing to get excited about. I make sure the sheet is cleated, check that the boom is secured so that it doesn't crash back and forth in the night, then I take in the quilt and stretch it out in the main cabin to finish drying. For a small moment I entertain the notion of sleeping in the cockpit so I can better hear any freighters that might plow over us in the night, but with no way to get out of a freighter's path, I think I'd rather die in my sleep. I head back down into the boat and as a precaution or out of habit, I don't know which, I close the companionway hatch and slide closed the lock bolt.

Boats are easy enough to get into. Once, in Djibouti, I got back to the boat to find Mom and Duncan had gone out, locking up the boat behind them. I didn't carry a key, but I just crawled in through a small open window in the bathroom. Head. That's what a bathroom on a boat is called. That's using your head. Hilarious. On passage, the only thing that would come through the windows is seawater, and on quiet nights like tonight, we'd leave the windows open. I must be feeling creepy because I check all the windows and leave only a tiny porthole open over the galley.

I should be more afraid of the freighters. Maybe I almost wish we'd get run over in the night.

SOMETHING WRENCHES ME from sleep. My body feels like it weighs twice as much as it does, like when your hand goes to sleep and it feels like someone else's. I try to lift my head and the muscles in my neck scream with pain. I drop my head back onto the pillow, hating what woke me from the escape of sleep.

A fragment of dream pokes at my conscious mind, a dream of a kiss that makes me want to wipe it off my mouth. It's Ty's kiss, but it's not Ty in the dream, it must be the pirate. Duncan is there too, and other people. I shiver and pull the blanket more tightly around me. Duncan in the dream is smiling, or he seems to be. I can't really see his face.

Awake now, I can't even bring Duncan's face to mind.

I think of the photo in the bottom of the go-bag and I wish I had it, that and a flashlight so I could see Duncan's face. I have a photo of Ty, but it's an old one from when he was in high school, and I don't think it looks like him anymore.

The air in my cabin feels suddenly close, like it doesn't have enough oxygen. My heart pounds, I can feel my temples bouncing with the pulse. And I've soaked my shirt with sweat. The blanket now restrains me, fights me, as I struggle to untangle myself. It sticks to my bare legs, and I claw it from me. In the pitch black, my cabin feels like a coffin.

I yank at the collar of my shirt, seeking air. With scrabbling fingers, I loosen the latches on my cabin window, pressing my face against the screen, gulping night air. The coolness from outside runs down over my face and the back of my neck. The drumbeat in my temple quiets. Breathe.

Now I feel like laughing, but I don't trust myself. What if I laugh like a crazy person? What if I am crazy?

I roll out of bed and find my way out into the main cabin. Briefly, I think that maybe Mom is gone and my heart resumes its race, but I find her with my hands, exactly like I've left her. I smooth her hair. Her forehead does feel warm. I loosen the quilt around her shoulders. She mutters, which makes me jump, but then she falls quiet again. Her breathing sounds quicker than it did in the day. Is it tomorrow yet? I reach under the quilt to her watch and slip it off her wrist. It's a good watch, with tiny illuminated dots so you can tell time in the dark. Duncan got it for her before we left on the trip, and a matching one for himself. He wanted to buy me one, but I said I wouldn't wear it. A quick and brutal image floods my mind of Duncan, his arms stretched out in flight, and yes, his watch, and the horrible way his skull disengaged before he disappeared over the side. I grip the watch, focusing on the tiny swimming dots. At last, my vision clears. It's five, thank God, almost morning. I strap the watch onto my own wrist. I will not go back into my cabin. Instead, I grab the quilt that I washed yesterday and wrap up in it on the seat next to my mother.

According to the time zones, it's still last night at home. Ty hasn't gone to bed yet; he probably isn't even home. Jesse is curled up in her pajamas, doing her nails, watching reality TV, microwave popcorn at the ready. Dad's watching TV too. He has the news on, but he's fallen asleep. He'll wake up in his chair in a couple of hours and stumble off to bed.

If I could call them up right now, what would I tell them? What would I say to Ty? *Hey, Ty. Met someone new, a pirate with big teeth and bad breath.* And to Dad. *Hey Dad, I ditched Mom on her watch and now she's half-dead. Duncan is totally dead. This is your big chance to be the hero.* With Jesse, I wouldn't get a word in. She'd be telling me about how her Mom won't let her wear the new shirt she bought because it makes her look like a whore, that her newest boyfriend wants her to get a tongue stud, that she might, that it blows her mom's mind, that tongue stud, she'll say, and then she'll laugh. I'll say, *Hey Jesse, talk about mind-blowing. I washed bits of Duncan's brain out of the cockpit. Worse even than the brain were the clumps of his hair with fragments of skin attached. Sticky.*

I draw the quilt over my head and rest my forehead on my knees. My fingers trace a sore on my shin, a new one, I guess, from cleaning up after the pirates. The scab is still soft, but I find the edge with my fingernail and pry it off my leg. I feel blood on my fingers.

I could say anything to them, and no one would really understand what it feels like. How could they? I'm not sure if I even know what I'm feeling. I should be crying more, grieving for Duncan, worried about my mother. I can't feel anything right now, not even the wound I've forced open on my shin. I lift my fingers to my mouth and taste the blood. I don't know why, but for an instant, I think I find the scab on my fingernail and put it in my mouth. I shudder and wipe my hand.

TEN

THERE'S A PALE LIGHT IN the cabin, and I heat a kettle of water on the butane stove to make tea. I can't find the teapot and the Thermos is gone, I know that, so I put the tea bag right into the kettle. The mug I take out to use is my mother's. The labeled letter "J" makes me think of washing dishes with Duncan and him asking me to stand watch with Mom.

I don't know what difference it would have made, me being there with her. What was I going to do, leap into the pirates' boat like a human sacrifice? They didn't even want me. They just wanted our stuff. I rummage in the cupboard for a container of sugar and find it open, the sugar like concrete with the exposure to the damp air. Using the handle of a spoon, I chisel crystals into the bottom of the mug, then pour the tea on top. I guess I could have stood between Mom and the bullets. They wouldn't have shot at her if she'd just stopped the engine. The first shots they fired didn't hit the boat. Like Mac said, they were warning shots. Maybe if I'd been out there, I could have calmed Mom down, I could have stopped her from firing the flare at them. What did she think, anyway, that a flare gun was going to stop them?

The tea tastes like tank water. Duncan liked to filter the tank water before making tea. The metal taste of the tea reminds me of blood, of Ty. It burns the back of my mouth and makes my eyes water, too hot to swallow but I do. Strands of sugar trace over my tongue.

I don't know what Duncan expected of me. Did he really think I could protect my mother?

I reach into the canned goods locker, selecting one without a label. I don't look at the magic-marker label. I heft it, trying to guess its contents. "Green beans." I check and I'm right. I toss the can back into the locker and pick another one. This one feels solid, like canned chili. I toss it back without reading the top. I want peaches, or canned pears, something in syrup that I can drink. I bring out another, shorter can. Pineapple. Bingo. This lid needs an opener, and I find one in the jumble of a drawer. Mom's labeled the can *pineapple tidbits* but it is actually rings. I hook a ring with my finger and eat it over the sink. I make myself eat all of the fruit before I tip the can to drink the juice.

The tea has cooled so that I can gulp it down. I'm hungry suddenly, totally ravenous. I wish for a fat pink ham, adorned with pineapple rings and red cherries like old ladies used to make. French fries and ketchup. Chocolate cake. A box of chocolate truffles dusty with cocoa. Normally, the canned goods locker is jammed to the top. There's maybe a dozen cans left. The eggs are gone, of course. We only had a few loaves of bread and these I'm sure went out when I was bailing. We probably have flour. I could make bread. Emma showed me how she does it in a heavy pot on the top of the stove. Maybe I could make a chocolate cake. Oh yeah, no eggs.

I lift the hatch that covers the fresh vegetable bin. We keep potatoes and onions in one, and it is still full. I peel open the plastic lid on another bin and find two heads of cabbage. Well, I'm not going to starve. The tomatoes we keep in a basket over the counter and these are gone, either by the pirates or the storm. Too bad. I find some apples but these have been rolling around inside a locker and already they smell sickly sweet with bruises. I pare the worst off one and eat it right down to the seeds. With the apples I find one of Mac's lemons. I hold it up to my nose and inhale. It's intensely lemon, far more so than lemons we buy at home, and bigger.

I never had any of that lemon pie.

I look over at Mom, on the dining bench. Her cheeks look flushed. Walking slowly, as if that will hide my concern, I take the lemon over to her. I hold the lemon under her nose. "You need to wake up."

I know what will wake her. But first, I pour tea into a water bottle and add a generous stream of sugar. If I'm hungry, surely Mom is too. At the very least she needs fluids. I shake the bottle until the sugar dissolves in the just-warm tea. Then I cut open the lemon and squeeze the juice into the tea.

I know what will wake my mother, and maybe I'm twisted, or maybe it's just what I have to do. I slip my arms under her quilt and yank her onto her back.

As her gunshot leg hits the bench her eyes snap open, and her mouth, and she sucks a breath. Moving quickly, so I don't have time to think too much, I haul her into a sitting position.

"Morning, Mom."

Her eyes well, and she moans, a horrible grunting moan that seems to rise from her belly and lodge in her throat. I can't stand the sound, the utter animal sound, but it comes and comes until I think I will cover my ears. Then she stops. Her eyes track vague circles around me.

I put the water bottle against her cracked lips. "Drink." She tries to close her lips, but I jab the bottle against her teeth. "Open your mouth and drink." She blinks and her eyebrows knot, but she drinks.

"Good." I show her the half-empty bottle. "You did really well. Maybe I'll make you some soup or something." She seems to be looking at me, but I can't be sure. "Would you like some soup?"

Her eyes slide under her lids until all that shows is white. "Mom?"

I put my hand on her forehead and snatch it away. "You're hot. Too hot." I rip the quilt away from her leg. The smell from her dressings makes me want to retch. The gauze fabric has crusted to her leg. I grab the teakettle and a towel that's still folded in the drawer. I can only hope that it's clean. Using a corner of the towel, I dip it into the kettle, then work it under the edge of the bandage. Carefully, a bit at a time, I remove the old bandage. The skin under the bandage is hot to the touch and red. Around one wound, the skin has puckered like a crater, and what was initially clear ooze is now yellow pus. It's infected.

My mouth goes dry, my mind goes blank. The first aid course I took echoes in my head. In case of infection, the victim needs medical attention. The victim needs a doctor. Call 9-1-1. I can't do any of those things! I listen to my mother's heart. It doesn't seem as fast as mine, but I can't be sure. Tears burn the corners of my eyes. I check my mother's pads. Except for one with a small, pungent spot, the pads are dry. So she's dehydrating too. I replace the one pad. With the cooled tea I clean the leg wound and cover it loosely with fresh gauze. I turn her so that she's laying on her other side and pull the quilt back around her. Wherever I touch my mother, heat comes off her in waves.

My own heart is racing and my hands are shaking. The infection probably accounts for her temperature. Her body is trying to fight it off. I pump a bowl of cool water from the tank and with another towel, sponge her forehead, chest, and back of her neck.

I gather the used towels into the bowl and take it to the sink. Yesterday I just threw out the bloody towels, but I'll have to wash these or I'll run out. If I heat water on the stove, I can boil them to kill any germs. When we left Djibouti, we had everything anyone could need on this boat. Both Mom and Duncan were crazed that way, packing and stowing and recording so that we could be self-sufficient, so that we could survive in a world without 9-1-1. And if we lost our boat, then the go-bag too had everything we needed to survive, at least for a while. My eyes go to the wall next to the stairs where we strapped the go-bag. The varnish is lighter where the bag used to be, a ghostly shadow in the exact outline of the bag.

I let the bowl clatter into the sink. They won't even know what half of the stuff is. They'll probably pitch out the antibiotics. They'll have a good laugh at the photo, telling their pirate friends how we tried to fight them off with a flare gun.

I put my hands up to my head. I know we had antibiotics in our big first aid kit, but the pirates took them or they're lost. And the go-bag, of course. I clench my teeth. Where else? Where else would Mom and Duncan keep antibiotics?

I slam open the door to the medicine cabinet in the head. I've already checked in here about two hundred times, but maybe they put some in another kind of container. I plug the sink and dump my mother's vitamins out. Just vitamins. Her birth control pills are here. She doesn't use them for birth control; Duncan had a vasectomy. Apparently, they help moderate PMS. She could use a stronger dose. There's a half-roll of Tums and a blister pack of seasick medicine, that's it. Under the sink I pull out more pads, a package of toilet paper, several cleaners, including antibacterial surface wipes that I set aside, a package of Velcro hair rollers my mother bought and never used, thank goodness, and my shower kit. I haven't used it since Australia. The marina there had showers so clean you could go in bare feet. In Australia, I washed my hair every day. I take a careful sniff of my underarms. Okay, so this is a different world. I put everything back under the sink, shovel the spilled vitamins back into the bottle and close the cabinet. There's a small cabinet in my mother and Duncan's cabin that I've checked, but I'll do it again.

When I open the cabin door, the smell of my mother's perfume hits me between the eyes. After the attack I wiped up their floor, but the scent has permeated everything in the cabin. Breathing through my mouth, I paw through their cabinet.

More vitamins. A small make-up kit with foundation, mascara and, wow, two shades of lipstick. Mom took this sailing minimalism seriously. Duncan's shaving kit, even under the onslaught of broken perfume, still smells like him. I zip it back up. Mom's kit has a tube of Tylenol that I keep, but nothing else that's useful. I dump out their drawers onto the bed. At home I used to hide things under my bottom dresser drawer. Sometimes I'd find stuff there that fell out of the back of a drawer and down the inside of the dresser. I get onto my hands and knees and feel around the inside of their cabinet.

Apparently, my mother knew about the hiding place as well, although the pirates missed it. In hers, I find a zipper bag with our passports and some cash and most of their credit cards. Another bag holds a picture of me, this year's school picture. In the picture I'm wearing a pale blue V-neck shirt. Jesse bought the same shirt and it looks better on her because she actually has cleavage. She said she forgot I bought it. At least she didn't get her picture taken in it. I don't have the shirt anymore. It got torn and I threw it away.

I wonder if Mom has this picture so she could show it to the authorities if I ever made a break for it. Like I would. Half the time I spent in the cities was within sight of the boat, reading a book in the shade of a building, or playing with the seawall cats. Not that I'd ever tell her that.

The bags are beaded with water, and I feel a small puddle in the bottom of the cabinet. I get right down on my belly and peer inside. A perfect circle of daylight meets my eye, a bullet hole in the side of the boat. Oh, good. The hole is above the water line, but in the storm the waves must have washed in. How many other holes like this are hidden behind the furniture?

There's one last bag, a small package inside wrapped in tissue paper. There's no card, but the tag is my father's handwriting: *For Lib, on your birthday.* The wrapping paper is the same he used on my Christmas gift that came while we still were in Australia. He must have mailed this one along with it.

My birthday isn't until April. Through the plastic I feel the package, tantalizingly heavy. What the hell. I open the plastic bag, pull out the gift and rip off the paper.

It's a folding knife, with a blue handle and a bright yellow cord. I open the blade. It has saw teeth, like Duncan's sailing knife he always carried in his pants. Duncan would have slept with his. It would be in the pants he was wearing when he went overboard. My temples pound.

So, it's a sailing knife. On it are tools I wouldn't know what to do with—a nail file, a small paring knife. I study each one, marveling at how much fits in one compact knife. As gifts go, it is definitely the most weird, but somehow, it pleases me.

A year ago on my birthday, I was grounded. Jesse and I had been at the mall and met some guys who were going in to see a movie. We went with them, without phoning, of course, and so were hours late getting home. Dad said that for my birthday he'd bake me a cake with a file in it like they used to do for convicts so they could break out.

This year, Mom would be happy if all she had to worry about was me being at a movie late. Using my new knife, I cut a piece of heavy-duty silver tape and plaster it over the hole in the hull. Won't hold out much, but it gives the illusion of repair. I leave the drawers pulled out so I can keep an eye on the hole, but I fold all Mom and Duncan's stuff neatly back into the drawers and stack them on the bed. I slip the yellow cord of the knife around my neck.

ELEVEN

NO ANTIBIOTICS. I grab the Tylenol tube and set it in the galley where I've put the rest of Mom's bandage supplies. To Mom I say, "Unless you have another secret stash somewhere, then we don't have any antibiotics. And if you *do* have a secret stash, then by all means, wake up and tell me where it is."

From the bruised apples I select a relatively healthy victim and take it and a foil pack of tuna over to the dining bench. With my knife I carve paper-thin slices of apple that I set onto my tongue, imagining that they are dissolving like snowflakes. I roll tuna inside the apple wafers and eat them together. The sweet crunch of the apple goes well, I think, with the salty blandness of the tuna. Surprising, really, that no one has thought of doing this before.

I open the saw-tooth blade of the knife. Duncan said his could cut through wire rigging if it had to. Mine would surely cut through fishnet. I would just have to dive under-water to the propeller. Dive under the boat.

I swallow.

"How hard could it be?" I direct the question to my mother. "I can put my head under water in the bathtub. I've done it in a pool. I just don't like to. That doesn't mean I can't."

I climb out into the cockpit. Outside, a light wind combs the jumbled seas into some sense of direction. The headsail is billowing loosely. My hair brushes my cheek. The knife hangs around my neck. I find a swim mask in the cockpit locker and fit it over my face.

It smells of old tires and seaweed and sucks on my face too hard because I forget or don't know that I have to breathe through my mouth. I don't seem to get enough air that way and I have to fight hard against a rising panic. I force myself to slow my breathing, make myself calm down, before I let myself take the mask off. I laugh a little, it's so stupid. It's just a face mask. I put it back on but push it up onto my forehead.

"I'll tether myself to the boat. That way, I can pull myself back up whenever I need to."

The waves stir the water to an opaque gray. Anything could be under there. "But there's nothing under there, and anyway, I can climb back onto the boat whenever I want to." I clip a tether to the wheel post. The tether extends just to the swim platform on the back of the boat. "Not long enough. I'll need to attach two together." Mentally I estimate the distance to the propeller under the boat. When Duncan bought the boat he had it pulled out of the water to inspect it. I know where the propeller is. I know that the bottom of the boat is painted black and looks like the belly of a whale. I didn't like standing under the boat when it was out of the water. I felt that it could trap me. I'm not thinking about what it will be like to swim under it. "Maybe I'll use three tethers, just to be sure." I link the tethers and make a loop in the end to slip under my arms. I can't wear the harness because it's designed to inflate when it submerges in water.

Duncan wasn't tethered. He didn't have a harness that would inflate to keep him above water. The image of his yellow jacket slipping under the water makes the breath stop in my throat.

"I can do this. I'll get the propeller free and start the engine. Then I can be out of here."

I sit at the edge of the swim platform and let my feet swing over the water. I tug on the tether, making sure it's secure. And again. I take the knife from around my neck and shorten the cord so that it hangs from my wrist. I open the blade.

"The ladder!" I get to my feet and unfold a two-step ladder that extends the short distance into the water. It's harder than it looks to get back on the swim platform without the ladder. Duncan tried it once just to see if he could do it. He couldn't. He had told us a story about these people who

were becalmed on a passage and decided to take a swim.
They all jumped in, then realized they'd forgotten to put
down a ladder. Their boat was found but they weren't.

Mom said it sounded like one of those urban myths. Still,
she always checked that Duncan put the ladder in before
he swam. On the few occasions they swam together, Mom
made me sit in the cockpit. Some lifeguard.

Duncan only told us those stories when we were still at
home. Once we moved onto the boat, real life was scary
enough. I yank on the tether one more time, check the ladder, pull the mask over my face, grasp the knife in one hand
and step down into the water.

It's not cold, but my breath blasts from my mouth in
gasps. I climb back onto the bottom rung of the ladder. I
can do this. I lower myself to my shoulders. Still gripping
the ladder, I plunge my face into the water.

The salt always surprises me. Cool water crawls over my
scalp, into my ears. I lift my face and gulp a breath, then
before I can think too much, I let go of the ladder.

The tether is taut and I let out some slack. Treading in
place, I swallow huge gulps of air. The swim platform bobs
above my head. From where I am, the hull of the boat seems
to curve endlessly under the water.

"So, I'll just dive under the boat now." My voice sounds
ridiculous with my nose sealed under the mask. Dibe udder
da boat. I suck in as much air as I can hold, then let go of
the tether.

Through the mask, the sea is green where the light
touches, then appallingly quickly, fades to black. I've barely

submerged and already my air feels spent. I pull my arms against the water and kick my legs. In air. My legs aren't even under water. The tether wafts around my shoulders. I could swim right out of it. I burst back to the surface for air.

I knot the loop in the tether so it holds snug against my chest. My skin is prickly with goose bumps. This time I use the bottom step of the ladder to push off.

Under the boat, there's no sunlight. Under the boat, the water is black. It meets me like a wall and I backpedal. The tether snakes around my legs. I don't have enough air. My eyeballs feel like they could burst. I struggle to swim out from under the boat. My foot brushes slime on the belly of the boat. When I break free of the water, I rip the mask from my face and yank huge breaths into my lungs.

I can't do it. I wasn't even close to the propeller. I could see the snarl of netting around it, an enormous dreadlock. It will take hours to cut free.

But when I cut it free, then I can start the engine. I have to cut it free.

I put the mask on, crying now. I dive and pull, pull harder, kicking against water now, kicking toward the black underbelly. Pull! I reach for the net.

The net is light and dense at once, like the inside of a golf ball, the way the strands of elastic wrap into a solid mass. I don't like the way the gossamer net wants to hold me. Wants to trap me.

My lungs are on fire. My throat contracts, trying to breathe. I stab at the net with the knife, slash it, then haul myself hand-over-hand up the tether.

It takes too long to surface. I want to breathe water. My back scrapes on the underside of the boat. Finally I'm breathing air.

Three more times I dive, pull myself to the propeller, stab and slash at the net, claw at the fibers and some come free. Bits of net waft in front of my mask. My eyes blur with the effort. I rake the knife across the net, plunge it into the net, again and again.

I need air so badly that my gut is pulling in and out, trying to find air. I can hear my blood pounding in my ears. When I can't stand it any longer, I turn to go up, and that's when I see him. Duncan. He's hanging suspended in the water below me, his head tipped up and wafting with the motion of the water, his gray hair streaming around his gray face. His eyes are open, gray and sightless, his mouth too. From the open side of his skull, gray tendrils trail from his brain. I scream. A school of black fish flee from beneath him, flee from their meal. I scream again and saltwater sears the back of my throat. I grab for the tether, grab and pull and kick, I don't take my eyes from him, but he disappears in the black water. I claw for the surface, break the surface. At first I can't draw air, then when I do, it forces my lungs against my ribs until they'll burst. I scramble onto the ladder, then onto the swim platform, then into the cockpit.

My breath comes in ragged bursts. My legs are shaking so I can hardly stand. Then I'm crying with shame and defeat. It was just my oxygen-deprived brain. I peer into the waves, struggling to get a glimpse of him again. He isn't there, never was.

TWELVE

In a movie, Jesse and I would laugh. First we'd scream, then we'd laugh. If I were writing the script, I would have Duncan extend his lifeless hand and grab my ankle. I shake off the image of the little black fish.

Wind has come up. Wind means we can move, even if I freaked out and didn't get the prop free. I tried again but only got as far as the bottom step on the ladder. Even when you know it's not real, scary stuff lingers, like after seeing a scary movie, when you check the closet and under the bed for a week. I spin the wheel, and the bow eases into a general northerly direction, close enough for now. I tighten the nut on the hub of the wheel to hold it in place, then move around in front of the wheel to adjust the genoa.

We have an automatic pilot on this boat but it uses battery power, a lot of power. Without the engine to charge the batteries, I don't have a lot of power, so I have to steer the boat myself.

The wind fills the sail and the boat heels and we lean away, not exactly at breakneck speed, but we're under way. The boom rockets back and forth against the mainsheet as if it too wants to take the wind. I settle on the cockpit bench next to the companionway and check the chart.

The Red Sea occupies the crack between the northeast edge of Africa and the Arabian Peninsula. Djibouti is at the south end, the Suez Canal into the Mediterranean at the north. The island of Masamirit is roughly halfway up and marks the turn toward Port Sudan on the African coast, about six hundred nautical miles from Djibouti. Our plan was to make Port Sudan where we could fill up with fuel and provisions, then make another passage to the Suez. Emma figured the passage to Port Sudan would take less than a week. Before the attack, when Duncan went off-watch, he marked our position on the chart. His precise pencil-marked circle indicates the time, 3:00 AM, the date, over two days ago, and our course and speed. A half-circle indicates where Duncan thought we'd be at that time based on calculations he did back in Djibouti. Emma and I plotted a similar line on her chart. It's called dead reckoning. I swallow. Talking out loud, I study the chart. "The problem is I don't know where we are now. Presumably, on Mom's watch she held the same course which put us, at the time of the attack, about here, two hundred miles into the trip and just north of Jabal at Tair Island." I mark a light X on the chart. "We could have moved a fair distance in two days just with the motion of the sea. What did Emma say about currents in this part of the Red Sea being in the same direction as the wind?" I struggle to remember, making quick notes on the side of the chart. "The storm was from the south, so blew us northward, and with the drift of the current, we might have made about two knots an hour, which is like saying two nautical miles an hour. That would put us well over one hundred miles south of Masamirit Island, and nowhere near Duncan's dead reckoning plot." I mark another X on the chart. Using a second pencil as a straightedge, I draw a line on the chart. "So to get back on course, we have to steer a line roughly like this."

Who is this *we*?

"I have to steer a course, a wild-ass guess, really, based on a wild-ass guess as to where I am now. A real sailor could use the sun and stars to find his position. Duncan has a sextant on board, although he never used it. He got our position from his GPS, which the pirates now have, including the spare GPS that Duncan kept in the chart table, and the one in the go-bag. I can't use the autopilot, so I have to steer twenty-four hours a day. And take care of Mom." I rub my sore neck. "I could aim for another port." Duncan has circled alternative ports on the chart, although some of these would be last resorts, literally, and with the reefs, dangerous for Emma to navigate, never mind me. In Australia

I saw boats up on the rocks, gaping holes in the sides from where the rocks bit through the thin hulls. I might make it off the boat, but I'd never be able to get Mom off. And then the shoreline might be uninhabited, or it could be days before anyone could get help. "My best bet is to try to get close to Masamirit where the others might be looking for me." I tap my pencil on the chart. "To get within range of someone who might come back for me."

One sail instead of two, and no engine—at this rate of speed, Mac and Emma will already be in the Suez. My throat aches with the futility of the plan. I tip my head back and close my eyes. The boom thumps against its restraints with each light breath of wind, but I can't be bothered to secure it. "I need to steer the boat, use the wind I have, don't let any spill from the sail." The sun feels warm on my face. "I'll do all that, sure." Below, I can hear Mom murmuring in her sleep. With the wind, the boat motion is less like being in a washing machine. Thump, bump, bump. I need to move the mainsheet block so the boom doesn't thump. Thump, bump, bump. It's not the boom. My eyes fly open. It's coming from the very back of the boat. I get up and move to the stern rail. Below me, on the swim platform, a locker door that holds our lifeboat canister is swinging open. The lifeboat canister is no longer in there, taken by the pirates, no doubt. The locker is always latched, but it isn't now, and that's what has been making the noise.

Okay, I'm certifiable now. I need to go and latch the locker door. I don't want a wave to take the door off, and

I sure don't want water in that locker acting as an anchor. But I'm afraid to go even as close to the water as the swim platform.

Every scary movie I've ever seen replays itself in slow motion in my mind. Duncan used to rent old classics like the one about the blind lady who went around loosening all the light bulbs so at night, the bad guy would be in the dark and she'd have the advantage.

Not much advantage, really, more like half a chance. She was just an old lady.

Then there was that Nicole Kidman movie where she and her husband are on a sailboat and the weirdo takes her hostage. I thought that movie was pretty funny, the way the bad guy, after they thought he was dead, climbed back onto the boat.

This is stupid. Just go and latch the locker door. He's not going to reach a cold bony hand over the swim platform and wrap it around your ankle and pull you into the water, under the water, down deep into black water, to the place of the dead.

The wind has increased substantially. The boat is carving a path through the water. Gingerly, I take a step down to the swim platform. Then another. I need to pee. The movement of the boat is greater here, like being at the end of the teeter-totter when it bumps on the ground. I'm suddenly aware that I'm not tethered.

Green water sloshes over the swim platform, dousing my feet.

Oh, here's a good one. *Jaws:* how the shark took out the

entire back end of the boat. Those big teeth strung with human entrails.

I crouch down and slam the locker latch in place, ripping skin off my knuckles, then stumble on the steps back into the cockpit, peeling another strip of skin off my shin. I'm breathing as if I'd run four times around the track. Back in the cockpit, only then, I look into the water.

There's nothing. I knew there wouldn't be. Right.

THIRTEEN

"WE'VE GOT SOME WIND NOW, MOM. We can sail." I don't tell her that I didn't get the prop cleared, that I was too afraid. I tuck a bottle of water into her berth, just in case she wakes up with miraculous strength and will to live. "And here's a pack of saltines, a little crumbly, I'm afraid."

I step in behind the wheel, loosen the nut and adjust our heading. Then I tighten the headsail. The boat heels as we pick up speed. If the wind comes up any more, I'll have to furl part of the genoa. A gust could knock us down.

I open a granola bar, pocketing the wrapper, nibbling the crunchy oatmeal in small bites. I have another in the pocket of my sweatshirt, but I make myself wait for it.

It's not easy steering the boat. With no land in sight, all I have to go by is the compass bearing. I try to make small movements with the wheel so that the boat doesn't yaw. Mom hates it when we yaw.

I hope she's all right. I hope she doesn't wake up and think she's alone. I'll have to get down below to check on her before it gets dark. Dark. I force panic back down my throat. What am I going to do tonight? I'll have to stay out here to sail the boat, but I know I won't be able to stay alert all night.

Emma could. She sailed single-handed once across the Atlantic. She said she slept in the daytime mostly, when freighters were more likely to see her and not run her down. She set her alarm so that she woke up several times an hour.

Of course, she had an autopilot that steered the boat for her. And she didn't have a mother on board with a festering, gunshot leg.

In the pirate movies, the ship's doctor was always saw-ing off infected limbs. I picture my saw-tooth knife, my mother's leg.

Mac could do it, maybe, cut off someone's leg, but Emma couldn't. Emma once, at the market, bought a fresh chicken, really fresh, because they plucked it for her but left its innards. She made Mac clean it. He grossed us all out by extracting the gut in a long gray strand.

The granola bar threatens to make a break for it.

I stand at the wheel all that afternoon, pretending that my legs aren't tired, pretending that the granola bar was enough to eat. Finally, I let myself go below for a break.

First, I prepare for the long night. I clean Mom's leg wounds using the anti-bacterial wipes I found earlier and cover them loosely with gauze. She's out again, which makes it easier to work on her leg. When she's conscious and I shift her in her bed, she cries out and often slips away, from the pain, I guess. But I have to move her so that she's not always lying on the same spot. I wash her with cool water and change her T-shirt. It's about all I can do and the effort seems pathetic. I pull the quilt around her shoulders. I dig out my foulies to wear in the cockpit: warm socks, boots, pants and jacket, along with a fleece cap and gloves. I may not need everything, but there's nothing worse than being cold. I glance over at Mom. Okay, there are worse things than being cold. I boil a pot of potatoes, cutting them up small so they cook fast, throw in some shredded cabbage and mash everything with milk. I put a bottle of hot sauce in my pocket because I can eat almost anything if it has enough hot sauce. I fill water bottles, pee again, then take everything to the cockpit.

The evening has already cooled. I set us back on course, then spoon out the potatoes. It's not even close to delicious, but it's food. I sprinkle my bowl with peppery sauce, place the bottle in the cup-holder on the wheel post, and settle against the stern rail to eat.

On the sea, the setting sun plummets from the sky, leaving a blaze of red in its wake, then blackness. The compass is dotted with luminescence, like Mom's watch, so that I can steer. I put the fleece cap on to ward off the night air. Even with all my gear, I shiver.

I try not to check Mom's watch. Time can creep so slowly at night and it feels awful to think an hour has passed when it's only been ten minutes. So I play a game with myself. When I want to check the time, I make myself mentally sing the lyrics of three songs, then I count to three hundred sixty. Sometimes I try to recite the alphabet backward.

Before, when it was Duncan, Mom and me, the most we'd be out here was three hours. The worst watch was midnight until three because the night was long on either side. Duncan usually did this one. That way, Mom could finish her watch as the sun came up. That's what happened when the pirates found us. When I had left her alone on her watch.

Tonight I'll do every watch. And tomorrow night, and the one after that. If that's what it takes.

The moon rises out of thin strands of cloud, startling me with its redness. With no power, we're traveling without lights. Normally all boats carry lights, in set colors and configurations to indicate the direction and size of the boat. That's how you know what you're seeing in the darkness, and if it's going to mow you under. For an eternal moment the moon is an enormous freighter on the edge of night and it makes my heart stop, first to think it would run us over, then to think it might rescue us. But it won't do either because it is just the moon.

Emma said her mother called full moons *bomber moons* from the war, meaning the bombers could easily see their targets. I never asked her, but I wish I did: was a full moon a bad thing, because the bombers could see the ground, or a good thing, because the bombs would fall where they were supposed to, on military bases and landing fields, not on apartment buildings and hospitals?

The moon lends some light to the cockpit, for which I'm grateful. It allows me to see the compass, which, strangely, I find I need to check less frequently. My legs anticipate the cross swells. I can close my eyes and feel the wind over my neck and cheek, hear it popping and fluttering in the genoa, sense our direction as surely as watching the compass needle.

It makes me less afraid, knowing that I can "see" the wind.

I let myself sleep ten minutes each half hour, tightening the wheel to hold our general direction, setting the alarm on Mom's watch to wake me. I sleep curled on the floor of the cockpit, up against the companionway so that if Mom wakes up, I'll hear her. I tether myself to both wheel post and companionway.

The alarm beeps in my ear like a gong, hauling me from sleep, to my leaden feet, to the sail and the wheel and the compass. I don't sit down, because I'll fall asleep. I stand. I practice ballet moves from when I was six and Dad took me to the community center for lessons on Saturday mornings, then brought me home and watched cartoons with me. Ballet moves are from my first life, life with Mom and Dad together. Ty is from my second life, Duncan's life. And this now is number three. I remember plot lines from books I read and capsulate them into book jackets. Then I pretend I'm the reviewer and assign stars for how good they are. The Nicole Kidman movie, if it ever was a book, gets negative two stars. When the watch beeps again, it means I can tighten the wheel and crawl off to sleep.

Thin blades of light pry under my eyelids, then a quick dance of light and dark that doesn't fit. I scramble to my feet. The genoa is flogging. "What have you done? You've changed our heading!" The wheel is still tight, the compass indicating that the wind has decreased with the dawn and changed direction. I sheet in the headsail but there is far less wind. I peel off my cap and jacket and throw them on the cockpit floor. My watch alarm goes off, and I jab at the button to silence it. Night slime coats my tongue and teeth. My shoulder is sore from where I was sleeping. I am capital *B* bitchy, and we're going nowhere fast.

"Nice work!" I yell at the wind. I estimate our boat speed at two knots, maybe two point five. If the current is with us, we'll be lucky to make five knots. That means by midday, we'll only be off-course by about fifty miles. Without a radio, we're invisible at five miles, less with the seas. They are never going to find us. I slump onto the cockpit bench.

Last night's potato bowl has crusted up nicely. Even so, my stomach growls. I say, "Some bacon and eggs, then? Or maybe a fluffy omelet? Pancakes to go with? Syrup? How about a GPS? Some proper medical supplies. *A radio?*" I peel off the rest of my foulies. My stink rises out of the layers of clothing.

FOURTEEN

BELOW, MOM'S FOREHEAD FEELS WARMER than yesterday. I go through the routine of caring for her, telling myself that it's not a charade, that she's strong enough to fight the infection, that people did it all the time before the invention of antibiotics. I leave her loosely covered and open the small porthole over her berth so she gets fresh air.

Her voice startles me, then scares me with its intensity. "Duncan," she says. "I need to see Duncan." Her eyes are wide, bright. She's looking at me, then her eyes close, and I think she's gone back under, but no, it looks like she's closing them against pain.

I make my voice cheerful. "Hey, Mom, you're just in time for breakfast. I can make you some broth, or how about applesauce?"

"Get Duncan."

"Let's start with some water. You need some water." I bustle around filling a water bottle, hoping on one hand that she'll stay awake long enough to drink, on the other hand, hoping she'll fall away before she asks again for Duncan. "Maybe you could handle some Tylenol if I broke it up a bit?"

Her eyes are on me now, watching my every movement, wild eyes. I bring her the water. "Try a sip."

She does, her eyes never leaving mine. "Now a bit of the Tylenol. It'll help with the pain and…" I stop before mentioning the fever. She already knows she feels like hell. But when I go to place the medicine in her mouth, she moves her head away from my hand.

"Duncan." It's a command. Her eyes are so clear, so intense right now that I have to look away. Big mistake. She becomes agitated, tries to lift her head, cries out in pain, then again, "Duncan!"

It makes me angry, her calling for him, and then I'm ashamed that I'm angry. I look her straight in the eye and the lie is out of my mouth with an ease that surprises me. "He's in the cockpit." Technically, he is, or parts of him, anyway. "We have to hand-steer because we don't want to run down the batteries, so he can't come in right now. We took turns steering in the night. He told me stories about the book he's reading, you know, the one about the woman pilot in Africa? I made him breakfast, and for lunch he's going to make fried rice. I like the way he makes it with hot peppers. We'll save you some for when you're feeling better. If it's not too rough this afternoon, he's going to work with me on that novel study. Maybe I'll use the book he's reading, although it isn't a novel, but the teacher won't care. She'll just be happy that I send it in, right? Ha ha."

Mom's eyes are closed. I know she's not sleeping, I can tell from her breathing. I see tears balling up at the edges of her eyes.

I'm too loud, and even to me my words sound fake. "You must be tired. You rest, and I'll check on you in a little while."

My mother always knows when I'm lying. It was a mistake to try. I grab what I need, my toothbrush, a clean T-shirt, hat, chart, the last of the granola bars and more water, then head back out into the cockpit. I'd like some tea, but what I want more is to get away from my mother's eyes.

I need to tell her about Duncan. She needs to know. But she's so weak right now. And if she knew that it was only me that was sailing the boat, she'd give up. Who could blame her?

FIFTEEN

I FOLD OPEN THE CHART and try to figure out where we might be by now. "Distance equals speed multiplied by time. Speed I can estimate, time I know. So distance is a whopping thirty-five miles from the last X." I mark the chart. I follow my finger toward the magic place, Duncan's original plot line, still hours and hours away. I shake off a sense of him watching over my shoulder.

At midday I get a pouch of tuna and a bruised apple. I eat the tuna first, then all of the apple, even the brown spots and the core, then I open the foil tuna package and lick out all the seams and creases.

I hope they're enjoying the corned beef, the bastards. Or maybe they've sold all our stuff and are wolfing down a twenty-dollar brunch at a white-cloth café. Wherever they came from, I wouldn't know. Except for a few words, I didn't recognize their language, and it seemed that they spoke more than one. In Djibouti, people from all over crammed the seaport: Somalia, Ethiopia, Yemen and the residual French population from when it was a French colony. On the main streets, the ones with wrought iron railings and American hotels, I heard French being spoken, and English, of course. English is spoken wherever there's a buck to be made from travelers. But on the back streets of the city among the poor, and there were so many of them, everyone spoke a different dialect. Whatever money there is in decaying Djibouti, the poor see none of it.

The pirates might have been from Djibouti or any of the Red Sea countries: Somalia, Yemen, Eritrea, Saudi Arabia, Sudan, Egypt. It's not like they flew their nation's flag on the stern of their boats. The boats were almost certainly fishing boats. Maybe, like Duncan said that night before we left, we turned up with them in the same square of sea, a floating buffet of unspeakable wealth. Ty ripped off Cokes from the 7-Eleven all the time. Said 7-Eleven was a "friggin' empire" and could afford it. "It's just a Coke."

Maybe they didn't intend to hurt us, they were just after our stuff. Maybe. They had their faces covered as they fired the warning shots; they didn't want to be identified. So they knew they were acting as criminals. What difference does it make that they have a day job? What kind of man blows the head off another, just to get his stuff?

The summer I was twelve I worked with Jesse's church group on a housing project on the lower eastside, in a neighborhood where no one was from where we were, geographically or socially or any way at all. Jesse signed up because she liked the pastor's son, and I signed up because she did. We spent two weeks pulling nails out of old lumber so it could be re-used. At the end of the first day, even though we had gloves, our palms were pebbled with blisters. We had water and juice and packed lunches, money for chips and Coke; we had everything we needed.

A little kid from the neighborhood used to hang around us while we were working, maybe five years old. His older sister kept an eye on him occasionally from the balcony of their apartment, like that would stop him from falling into a construction hole or wandering into the path of a cement truck. One day, Jesse gave him her Coke, and he vanished, reappearing on his balcony with his older sister and a horde of siblings, all clamoring for the Coke. The older sister took a good long swallow, then another, watching us all the time. Then she handed it to another kid. By the time it got back to the little boy Jesse had given it to, there would have been a few drops left. He didn't get mad though; he looked happy enough to get the small amount that was left.

The pastor told us that in one country he went to, if you brought supplies to a village to build a new well, the bricks and mortar might end up in one family's possession if the village deemed that the one family needed the supplies more than the village as a whole. The village is happy for the one family. In that country, the people have a different concept of need. It's not wrong, the pastor said, just different.

Apparently, the pirates too have a different concept of need.

Jesse and I hated the kid's older sister. And Jesse never did hook up with the pastor's son. I thought it was the hardest two weeks of my life.

Not anymore.

"My problem," I say, "is that I don't know where I am, and so I don't know where I'm going." I look behind me at the sea. "And I'm going too slow. I need the engine. With the engine, Mom and I have half a chance."

For the engine, I need to clear the propeller. I have to. It's that simple.

I attach the tethers. I open the knife. I put the ladder down. I spit in the mask, which I remember Mac doing, I have no idea why. "Hey Mac, wish you were here." Then I slip into the water.

With the boat moving, however slowly, there's an unpleasant sensation of the tether being tugged. I visualize myself hacking off the net in one superhuman swipe of the knife. Okay, maybe two.

When I put my face in, the salt of the water feels abrasive. I ignore it. I dive.

It is harder than yesterday, I'm not imagining it. I'm almost out of breath when I reach the propeller, barely able to attack the net before I have to return to the surface. But I'm not afraid. Today, I won't be afraid.

I dive again and again. There's water in my ears. My right shoulder is especially painful, so I switch the knife to my left hand and hack away.

The first time I feel it, I think it is strands of the net wafting around my legs. The second time I feel it, I know it's not the net. I push off from the net ball so hard that I crack my head on the bottom of the boat. A dorsal fin has brushed the back of my legs.

SIXTEEN

SCREAMING UNDERWATER IS USELESS. The ensuing gulp of seawater explodes out of my nose, loosens the mask, which fills and burns my eyes as I claw myself to the surface. My foot slips on the ladder, which rakes open the sore on my shin; my arms bleat with weakness as I try to climb the ladder; but I only feel any of this instantaneously because all I'm really thinking about is that fin.

I hear it behind me in the water, a sound I've heard before. It's a popping sound mixed with a whoosh, a sound a dolphin makes as it breathes. Dolphins! I haul myself onto the swim platform and turn to see them just as they dive under the boat.

There are four dolphins, then a set of three and another; they're so fast it's hard to count them. They are gray with a white banner flash on their sides, and some tip a little on their sides for a better look at me before scooting under the boat.

We first saw dolphins in the Indian Ocean. Mom was on watch and she called to Duncan and me to come see. There was a pod of about twenty, diving in threes and fours over our bow wave, under the stern, then back to the bow. They stayed with our boat for close to an hour and almost all that time I leaned over the rail, entranced. Duncan too. We marveled at their synchronized jumps, their sleek bodies breaking the waves at the exact same time, leaping eight, ten feet in the air, then back under the water, like at Marineland but so much better because these dolphins were doing it just for themselves.

I wanted to go forward on the bow to watch them. We have jack lines rigged all the way to the bow so we can attach a tether if we have to go forward, like how people sometimes clip a dog leash on the clothesline so the dog can run the length of the yard and not get away. Duncan said no, that there was no reason to go forward, and why take a chance on going overboard? Even with the tether, it would endanger everyone to get me out of the water.

It pissed me off and I'm sure I told him so; there are a few words in my vocabulary I used only on Duncan. So I stomped off and went below. I was glad when the dolphins left us that day because it meant none of us was seeing them. I imagined that they left out of solidarity for me, although it took them a while.

On one of my afternoon watches when I was alone in the cockpit, I heard a dolphin make that pip noise behind me. It was just one dolphin that I saw, and he dove under the boat and disappeared. I think he saw me and said hello, but I guess he could have been saying, "Get out of my way!"

Today, crouched on the swim platform as I am, these dolphins are so close I can smell fish on their exhaled breath. They shoot under the water like gray arrows, their dorsal fins knifing the water into ribbons, shooting back under the swim platform so that I could touch them if I leaned out.

In the Indian Ocean, that time with Mom and Duncan, one dolphin kept pace with us, tipped onto his side to watch our faces as we leaned over the rail. I outstretched my hand, and he veered away, then dove out of sight. I'd crossed some line of non-verbal communication and had broken the spell.

But today when I was under the boat, one touched me. It must have meant to swim so close to me that it touched me. It wouldn't have been accidental. Which one? I study the dolphins as they circuit the boat. I imagine the youngsters discussing it. "You touch her." "No, you."

How long did they swim with me before making their presence known? Did Mom hear their pips and squeaks through the hull of the boat, through her deep deep sleep? Did she hear what I, wide-awake, couldn't?

The sun is hot and except for my braid dripping water down my back, I'm already dry. Part of me nags about having to work on the net. Right now I'm content to watch the dolphins.

It doesn't bother me so much now, the thought of diving under the boat. The dolphins seem like company. Not that I'll jump in with them. For one thing, it'll spook them and they'll disappear. Then there's that urban myth about dolphins and drowning swimmers, the one in which the swimmer is rescued by dolphins that push him in to shore. As Emma might point out, we only hear about the rescued; we'd never hear from the swimmer who got pushed further out to sea.

If nothing else, with all this dolphin activity there's not another fish of any kind anywhere near the boat.

Most of the pod leaves, but three stay with me until the salt has dried white on my skin and even my hair is mostly dry. I miss them when they don't reappear, and for a long time I wait, hoping they'll return. When I can avoid it no longer, I climb down to the swim platform, onto the ladder, then slip into the water.

I'm making progress on the net, but it has wreaked enormous havoc on the propeller. In full motion, the prop spun the net into a dense fat rope, then twisted the rope around and around on itself. I have to cut through the tangled strands layer by layer, the knife not being big enough, or me strong enough, to saw through the entire thickness.

I got my hair caught in a hairbrush once, the round metal kind. I got scared when the brush wouldn't come out and managed to snarl my hair so badly that Mom spent an hour trying before she reached for the scissors. I begged her not to cut my hair, probably promised that I'd be good forever if she didn't. So she took me to a hair salon where two of them worked the whole afternoon to ease the brush out.

Sorry about breaking the promise, Mom.

I think about the dolphins and the power in their bodies that so easily challenges the resistance of the water. I don't have it. I am a land creature and the water repels me like oil, driving me back to the surface. I'm using most of my strength just to reach the propeller.

When the dolphins jump clear of the water, is it just momentum that carries them high into the air, or do they somehow swim through the air? Surely it's more difficult for a dolphin to overcome gravity than it is for me to overcome buoyancy. I envision the dolphins as human swimmers, long hair streaming over smooth, strong shoulders, bodies lithe and sleek. When Mac dives, he uses just his fins to propel himself, and I've seen him kick with his feet together just like the dolphins, a smooth, undulating up-and-down motion that seems to start under his ribs and ripple from his feet. Now I see Mac as a dolphin, and I shake my head to clear the image.

If I could pull myself down to the propeller…

Use a jack line. The answer comes to me just like that, as if a sympathetic classmate whispered it in my ear as the teacher tapped her fingers. Use a jack line, a long line from the ladder to the propeller, use it like a handrail that I can pull myself along. I detach the tether at my end and loop it over the others so that I'm attached to the line of tether instead of the boat. The unclipped end I will have to secure at the propeller. In the meantime, I clip it at my waist so that I'm still connected with the boat. I take a big breath, then dive.

The tether just reaches the propeller, and I loop it around the shaft and clip it onto itself. Then I pull myself back to the surface. I risk a small smile. This is going to work. Using the tether as a jack line, I haul myself easily downward to the propeller. Once there, I anchor myself with one hand holding the net and my feet braced on either side. This way I can use the knife like a saw. The diving is actually a relief. It's the constant pressure of the knife that burns from my fingers through my wrist and elbow then radiates in my shoulder and neck. Every two dives, I switch the knife to the other hand.

The net ball is loosening in reluctant strands. I leave these in place, pulling on them to find the path of the snarl. Sometimes a good length comes free, and I reward myself with a rest on the ladder. I can see the edge of the propeller blades now.

The sun slips toward evening when I crawl up into the cockpit. My hands are raw from pulling on the net. I'm sore from the bottoms of my feet to the top of my head. I drain a bottle of water, then rip into the granola bar. Then I go below to check Mom. She's out, but I talk to her as if she can hear me. "You wouldn't believe where I've been," I say as I wash her and change her dressings. "Under the boat. Remember when you signed me up for swimming lessons and I stood in the shower until each lesson was over?"

I dump the can of chili into a pan and set it on the flame. I'm so hungry that my hands are shaking, and I don't wait for it to get heated through. I eat it just warm, right out of the pan, then clean the pan with my fingers.

"Dad gave me a knife. It makes me feel good, like he trusted me to use it, not just that I wouldn't cut myself, but that I could actually use it like a tool. That I'd know what to do with it."

Mom is so not with me. I hold the knife out as if she is looking at it.

"I'm not making any sense, I know. But that's the way I see it. Dad knew I could do this. Maybe he didn't know that I could dive under the boat, but he knew I could figure out something that would work. He gave me the cake with the file in it." Mom's breathing is quiet, her closed eyes a door between us. "Anyway, I need to get back to work. I don't want to be under the boat if the wind comes up." I rinse the chili pan with a little water. "I need to finish what I started."

It's harder than this afternoon. During that brief break my muscles have set like concrete. I can barely close my hands around the knife. The tether has rasped my skin raw and when I dive, the salt water sears every tiny scratch. So that I don't feel it, I count, sometimes backward, sometimes in French; sometimes a manic drill sergeant pounds along beside me, screaming in my ear, *Hut, two, three, four, saw-the-net-and-do-some-more.*

I may be crazy, but I don't remember when I've felt saner.

Closer to the prop, the net is wound more tightly, which makes it easier to saw, almost like wood—almost. It's more like sawing a telephone pole with a handsaw. My knife blade is wearing dull, and I have to work harder to cut through the tough fibers of the net.

I don't know how many times I dive down, maybe fifty, maybe one hundred. And then it's done. A final length unwraps from the shaft, and when I drop it, spirals down, down, down and away. I detach the jack line from the prop and follow it one last time to the surface.

SEVENTEEN

THE ENGINE SEEMS LOUD AFTER the quiet of not having it. I lean across the cockpit bench and check the RPM indicator. I keep the throttle at about twenty-four hundred RPMs, fast enough for speed, but not so fast as to use up all our fuel. In contrast to the last couple of days, it feels like a giddy pace.

At first when I tried to start the engine, it turned over but too slowly to catch. Then I remembered to switch to the starter battery. It was that fast, my remembering, and the engine started as smoothly as if it had just been waiting, saying, *Come on, what's taking you so long? Let's get out of here!*

The engine means I can charge the battery, which means I can use the autopilot. I can leave a soft light on in the cabin. When I need to go below, I can take my time, prepare something to eat, check Mom. Check and check and check Mom. Sometimes her sleep seems almost normal, and I swear she stirs when I touch her. Other times, it's like she's dead.

When I got out of the water after clearing the prop, I rewarded myself with a hair wash. I used the shampoo from my kit and worked it into my hair, wetting it with more seawater, lathering it up into a good foam, then rinsed it in more seawater. Finally, I ran a couple of cups of fresh water through my hair to take out the salt. It's dry now and feels glorious, like salon hair, everything being relative.

I've put on my warm pants, and from the pocket I extract the remaining cookies in the Hobnob package. "Duncan used to love these too. At home he'd buy the kind with chocolate on one side, but it's too hot here for chocolate. It would just melt and make a mess." I take another bite. "His brain made a real mess, but I'm not going any further with that because I don't want to waste my Hobnobs."

"Duncan used to buy these cookies at the little store on the corner." I wave the package at my imaginary audience. "He loved that store. He said it was like all the stores used to be when he was young: friendly, small, where they knew you by name. From the woman who owned the store he bought curry paste that he'd bring home in a small jam jar he saved for the purpose. She mixed it for him the way she liked it. He cooked curried prawns once that were so hot they made Jesse cry. She actually wiped her tongue with paper towel." I finish the cookie and dig for another. "Mac eats fries with his curry, mixes them all up together. So gross. When Duncan cooked a curry, we always had ice cream for dessert to cool everything down. Duncan loved maple walnut ice cream. I'd eat it, but only if that's all that was left. My favorite ice cream is mint chocolate chip." I inspect the cookie package. "There's one left." I offer it to the air-guests but no one bites.

"The thing with maple walnut is that the nuts scrape your tongue, not so much if you eat it with a spoon out of a bowl, but from a cone, which is how ice cream is meant to be eaten anyway. Spoons just get in the way. With ice cream, what you're after is total tongue contact."

I wonder if Jesse got her tongue stud. Maybe she just got a new boyfriend. Jesse is practical that way.

Jesse says she can tell if the relationship is going to work the first time she kisses a guy. Not sparks, she says. That's just physical. She says she can sense a guy's soul through his lips.

Maybe. I don't know how much you can believe from someone whose longest "relationship" has been three weeks and that was only because she didn't want to break up with the guy on his birthday. She's a humanitarian, that Jesse.

Ty doesn't spend a lot of time kissing, not anymore.

"Nothing like savoring the moment." I empty the crumbs from the package into my mouth then fold the plastic into my pocket. My hands are stiff from hacking at the net and I rub them like those wrinkly women in the Advil commercials.

With the engine, I can run the lights; I can see when I go below. I can run the bilge pump, which is good because with our increased speed we're taking on some water, probably through the bullet holes in the hull. I can't charge Mom's handheld VHF radio because I can't find the charging unit. I'm not sure if any of the ships I see as distant shapes would respond to my radio call. It would be nice to try.

Could be I lost the charging unit when I bailed in the dark. Could be my fault for that too.

Tough to follow the trail of mistakes I've made. At first, Mom blamed my disasters on Jesse. She never said as much, but I could tell. It took Mom a while to abandon the idea that by being her daughter I was, by default, damn near perfect. Her first clue might have been my dumping Vanessa at the beginning of seventh grade, my best friend from even before kindergarten. My mom and Vanessa's mom are still friends. I'd still be friends with Vanessa except Jesse doesn't like her. Then there were the calls from the school: "Lib wasn't in math class today." "Lib missed her science test today." "Lib's in the office waiting to be picked up. She's suspended for lighting up in the girl's change room."

Vanessa doesn't even recognize me anymore. Maybe she does, and it's just easier for her to pretend she doesn't.

Then there were the guys at the mall, the ones we met last year before my birthday. Jesse had hers picked out from the minute she spotted him at the food fair. She assigned me mine, my first *date*, a tall guy with little pimples where his forehead met his hair. He was fairly nice, didn't try anything in the movie. He ate all my popcorn, and Jesse's too. She told me to hold it for her, that she'd be right back, she and the guy. I didn't know then where she was going.

I always wait for Jesse. Once I waited with one of her boyfriends while she hooked up with someone else in the other room. They're always nice guys, Jesse's boyfriends. Sometimes I almost felt bad for them.

Jesse doesn't always wait for me, though.

And the thing with Jesse is she is never wrong. Ever. She used to have a dog, Jesse did, a taut, wiry thing called Bree. Jesse got her when she first moved here in fifth grade. We used to take her for walks, Vanessa, Jesse and I, down onto the bog trails. We had to cross a set of train tracks, and Jesse never kept Bree on her leash. One time Bree ran out ahead of us just as we heard a train whistle, and she stopped right on the tracks. She was wagging her tail, and if she saw the train, she didn't know what it was. She was still young, practically a pup. Vanessa ran for the dog and I followed her. This scene plays out in stop-time and I couldn't invent it, no one could. Vanessa stumbled, caught herself, then stumbled and fell, right onto the tracks. I know she fell on the tracks because I heard the *clink* of her eyeglasses on the rail. I guess I screamed. The dog was still wagging her tail. The train whistle was screaming, that I know, one long, drawn, pleading blast, and I reached down for Vanessa. It's true what they say about having more strength when you're desperate. I yanked Vanessa clear to her feet, yanked her so hard she left the ground. The train was just three yellow lights, on us now, compressing the air in front of it so that at first it was hard to breathe, then the air punched to the bottom of our lungs, making us gasp.

What I was thinking right then was, *Oh no, Jesse is going to see her dog get killed.*

She didn't. As Vanessa and I moved back from the train, the dog bounded off the tracks toward us. Jesse caught her collar. The train finally came to a stop a ways up the tracks, but we didn't stick around. We ran, and Vanessa started to laugh, but I'm thinking that was just so she wouldn't cry. Or maybe so I wouldn't.

Jesse told me later that it was Vanessa's fault the dog was on the tracks, that she shouldn't have chased the dog. That Bree thought she was playing.

About six months after that, Bree got out of the yard and took off. Jesse said that she probably found a good place to live and more power to her; if she came back, then fine. The dog never did.

EIGHTEEN

I'M USING THE HEADSAIL WITH the engine. The sail provides additional propulsion and makes me more visible in case anyone on those ships is keeping watch. We always assume they're not, especially at night. So I'll repeat last night's routine: stay in the cockpit, stay awake, sleep only the brief ten-minute intervals in each half hour. I'm not looking forward to it, but at least we'll hold our course.

No clouds tonight and the sky is so dense with stars that I could reach up and run my hand through them. Nights like this would captivate Duncan. On our passages in the Indian Ocean he used to regale us over breakfast with the constellations he'd identified the night before. South of the equator the stars are different from at home, not that I'd know any, other than maybe the Big Dipper and the North Star, simply because the dipper points right at it. I always think of that song about following the drinking gourd; the one the slaves sang so they'd know which way was north if they tried to escape. One small reference point in a night as big as any ocean, that's all they had to go by. It's strange, in a way, how in order to find freedom, they had to go farther from home. Duncan used to show me the constellations, but I had difficulty following the patterns and it didn't excite me, which I'm sure I let him know. He used his binoculars to look at the stars. Mom said it made her feel unwell just to watch him doing it. Still, she often sat out in the cockpit to keep him company.

Duncan says the desert is like a sea, and that nomadic people still use the stars to find their way.

I wonder what it must have felt like for those enslaved people, when they finally reached America, to find that even the night sky was foreign.

Tonight, the boat curls the seas behind us and the prop stirs phosphorescent purple streamers that cling briefly to our trail. Yes, Duncan would like a night like this.

At first I think I imagine it, a quick movement of air across my cheek, but then the bird returns, fluttering over the cockpit before settling on the bench. It surprises me, its sudden presence, but I stay perfectly still, watching it just from the corner of my eye. It's small, the size of a sparrow, plain-colored plumage, a beak like a robin's. Duncan would know what kind of bird it is. He kept books on them. The bird watches me too, eyes like black pearls. Then it stretches out its wings, and I see a bright patch of yellow feathers appear beneath each wing.

It makes me smile, the way it holds its wings out from its body like that. It looks like kids do when they're pretending to be a bird or a plane. Maybe it's tired and is airing out its under-wings.

I often see birds overhead. The Red Sea is just a narrow neck of water between the continents, an easy passage for birds. In the Indian Ocean we rarely saw birds, and it always made Mom sad thinking they'd been blown off course in a storm. One landed on our boat and proceeded to devour a crop of little flies that had also found us and were scurrying around on the deck. The bird stayed with us all that afternoon then disappeared. Emma and Mac said they'd been visited too.

This bird has barely moved since landing. Occasionally I see it rearrange its tiny clawed feet for a better grip on the slippery cockpit bench.

Speaking quietly, I say, "You are one desperate bird if you think I can take you where you need to go." The bird tilts its head, almost like it is listening to me. "But you're welcome to come along."

The bird sways with the swells of the sea, sometimes splaying its tail feathers for balance. A couple of times it flutters up in the air but comes down again to perch on the bench. It's impossible to tell from the bead-like eyes where the bird is looking, but it is a wild thing, and it must surely be looking at me. How could it know that I'm not going to snatch it up in my jaws? What mental process happens in a wild thing's brain that allows it to accept greater risk in order to save itself? "Don't worry little bird. I've had enough of death."

Fanny would have a different notion of what to do with this bird. Her sharp cat teeth would be chattering right now and she'd be licking her lips.

The alarm sounds on Mom's watch indicating I can rest, and both the bird and I jump. This makes me laugh, and I imagine the bird laughing at itself too. I say to it, "It's your turn to keep a lookout. Let me know if you see a Pizza Hut." I settle onto the bench, lay my head down and curl my legs up. Maybe it's the bird being there, it's bright black eyes on me, but I don't feel sleepy. I turn onto my back and look up at the sky. The stars seem liquid, like quicksilver. I imagine sailing through the stars, pale moons and greenish blue planets like beacons guiding me through the night.

Quicksilver is mercury. Mercury makes you crazy.

If I moved closer to the bird, would it move away from me? Does it allow me only this prescribed closeness, no more, like lines of latitude that never touch? The other lines, longitude, they meet at the poles. They're really far apart at the equator, but at the ends of the earth, they converge to one ink dot, one point where they are no longer separate. If you stood in that very spot, would you be connected to the entire globe?

Emma would probably say that any spot on the world is connected so long as you can draw a line from it. She'd illustrate her point with an elaborate geometric design, showing how even independent spots are carried on lines whether they like it or not, and everything connects, given time.

When Duncan first moved in, I never spoke to him. If I had to ask him for something, like the salt, for example, I'd do it through Mom. "Mom, could you ask Duncan to pass me the salt." On the phone to Jesse, I'd talk loudly about what a jerk Duncan was.

Jesse liked Duncan because he always asked how she was doing, and he'd drive us anywhere, even if we phoned for a ride late at night.

I could feed this bird, and given time it would let me touch it. It would sell its wild soul for the easy life, even if I caged it. If I caged it, then I could do anything to it.

Maybe Jesse was right to let Bree go.

But I wouldn't cage the bird. I'd be happy enough to know it was staying with me because it liked my company.

Duncan used to laugh at my jokes. Mom never got them. We liked the same books. I allowed him only a prescribed distance and he respected that.

I know Duncan never bothered me at night. Mom was right. I wanted him to be a monster so I'd be justified in hating him. I don't know why I wanted to hate him. Maybe I thought that if I liked him I was betraying my father, that I was saying it was okay what my mother did, leaving my father, divorcing him. I close my eyes against tears.

I thought that if I hated Duncan enough, then my mother would too.

I'm sorry. I'm sorry I said what I did. I didn't let you get close and now time has run out.

When the alarm goes off again, the bird is gone.

NINETEEN

"Mom, I can't understand what you're saying!"

Her skin is flushed red and her shirt is wet from sweat, but she's shivering. Her eyes are glass.

"Maybe it's best if you just stay quiet. Try another sip of water."

Mom turns away, but I set the water bottle against her lips and trickle water into her mouth. I don't know how much really goes down, but I'm afraid to give her too much in case she chokes. I'm not sure she has the strength anymore to cough.

Normally, daybreak on a passage is the best time of the day, a victory over the long night, a hopeful, optimistic time of day. Not this morning. This morning, Mom's leg wound is strangely pale, the discharge now almost gray. I have to keep speaking to her, keep tapping her feet to make her stay awake so she can drink.

"You're giving up! You're choosing him again!" I pinch her foot, hard, and her eyes fly open.

"Oh, Lib, are you all right?"

I hear it, I know I do, but it's like when someone wakes up in a dream, my friend Vanessa would do that, just speak out like she was awake, but she wasn't. Mom's eyes are closed again, and nothing I do makes her wake up.

"No, I'm not all right and neither are you. We're in trouble." I swipe the tears away from my eyes. "And I'd just like you not to die. Okay? Do you think you can do that?"

I remember my mother doing the same thing to me after the party. She pinched my feet and it pissed me off. I just wanted to sleep. I could hear her crying, heard Duncan's voice saying, "He's gone and no one saw anything," then their voices low, angry and sad at once. There was some blood on my legs; I must have started my period. I let them turn me on my side in the bed "so she doesn't choke if she vomits." I let them pull the blankets around me. Then they left me alone.

I was in their bed.

"I know you can hear me, so listen. I'm sorry I lied about Duncan. I thought it would upset you if I told you the truth. I'm not real crazy about being without him myself." Mom's eyelids are veined in blue. Her hair needs washing. Her lips are cracked. "But you have to get over it, just for now, and when we reach Port Sudan, then we can have a good cry."

It's like she's a different person, this sleeping mother, like she's already left me, is in that mythical tunnel, gazing at the bright white light.

"*Mom!*" I shake her, hard, and her eyes widen briefly, then settle closed again. "Don't give up!" She is so stubborn. "Don't even think about leaving me alone." But it's no use. Her jaw slackens and she's out again.

Her breathing is fast, her pulse too. She barely managed the tiny amount of water I trickled into her mouth. I can't take a chance on her swallowing the Tylenol, so I put it under her tongue. Now I wait with her while it dissolves to make sure it doesn't go down her windpipe.

"No, Mom. I'm not all right. I'm doing the best I can, but it's not enough. I don't know where we are. We could be plowing toward the reefs for all I know."

With the headwind, the seas are short and steep, and I've had to sheet-in the headsail so the boat is heeled over, making everything tilt. Walking in the boat is like being in a manic fun house with the floor suddenly dropping away, then slamming my knees up to my ears, over and over. My hips are bruised from constantly banging into things. My arms are tired from hanging on for every step. In the cockpit, I can balance on my feet behind the wheel, and it's better, because I can anticipate the movement. But my thighs and calves feel like I'm in an aerobics class in hell.

I pack towels on either side of Mom's head to keep her from rolling too much in her berth and bunch pillows along her sides. Except for her T-shirt and shorts, I leave her uncovered. If the Tylenol does anything for her fever, I can't tell. I leave her leg wounds uncovered too, thinking that it might be good to let the air at them.

Sweat is already beading on her forehead and I wipe it away with a cool cloth. "I told you what I thought you needed to know, Mom. I'm sorry. I'm sorry about what happened to Duncan. I'm sorry you won't have him, that I won't have him." I have to pause a moment until the lump clears my throat. "I think Duncan was a good man, and I know he loved you. I think he even loved me, in spite of how hard that must have been. I miss him too, not just because I'm on my own to find our way off the sea. I miss him because he was good for us." I rinse the cloth, wring it and drape it over her forehead. "You and I would never have taken this trip without Duncan. However it ends, we tried. You tried, Mom, remember that. You did your best with me. I just wouldn't let you win. I thought that if I did, then that meant I was losing. But I was losing all along." I empty the bowl of water and hang up her towel. "Anyway, it was nice talking to you."

I tidy the galley, toss out the few remaining apples that are almost mush now, anchor the dishes in the cupboard so they don't make such a racket in these waves, and maybe I am losing it: I rearrange the glasses so that the labels all face out. *Duncan was here.*

I'm still finding shards of eggshell. This one has hardened onto a ceiling panel and I scrape it off with my thumbnail. I straighten up the bookshelves, throwing out some that have grown a fast black mildew from being put away wet. One of these is my math text, too bad about that, right, and a fat novel that was next on my reading list for Language Arts. I decide to put it in the cockpit anyway, maybe try to read a few chapters before it gets dark. That's one thing about fiction, the characters always have it way worse than the reader. Right. I make some tea and fry up some leftover potatoes with an onion.

I find three birthday candles in the cutlery drawer and light them from the gas ring. The tiny flames remind me of dolphins. I anchor them on a plate and rest the plate in the sink. I'd like to put them closer to Mom, but I don't want to set the boat on fire. The angels will have to find her.

TWENTY

I DON'T BOTHER WITH A PLATE, just take the whole pan up to the cockpit. Fine reddish sand, windborne for hundreds of miles from the northern deserts, dusts the cockpit. I have to put my back to the wind so I can eat. Even so, the potatoes take on a gritty edge. I drain one water bottle after another.

I've increased the engine speed and we're cutting through the waves, heeled against the headwind, the genoa catching what it can to increase our speed. I imagine what it would feel like, driving full-speed onto a rocky shoreline in the pitch black of night. I also imagine the silence of the engine if I run us out of fuel while we're still in the middle of the sea. Mostly though, I imagine my mother turning cold, but I try hard not to think about this because thinking it might make it real.

Reading was optimistic. I read the same page over and over and still don't retain a word. My eyes are constantly pulled to the horizon, to the endless water.

It is possible that I've overshot Port Sudan and that I'm motoring northward into oblivion. No one would look for me there and I'd run out of fuel and fresh water long before I reached the Suez.

I grab the chart. "The wind is from the north now, which means we're probably close to halfway up the Red Sea. The north wind against us means the current probably is as well and I can knock a couple miles an hour off of the engine speed. If we're that far north, then I should be seeing this island, Masamirit." But I'm not. All I see is green water and whitecaps. Masamirit is the turning point. From Masamirit, Duncan has penciled in careful course changes to make Port Sudan. "Masamirit has a light, according to the chart, so I should be able to see it night or day. But what if the light isn't working? Emma said lights in the Red Sea aren't one hundred percent reliable, or was it Duncan who said that? What if I sailed by Masamirit in the night and didn't realize it?" My throat begins to ache. "What if I'm too far east or west? According to the chart, the light on Masamirit has a range of ten miles. What if I'm just out of range and can't see it?" I jam the chart under the seat where it won't blow away. "I don't know why I bother with the chart. I may as well be sailing with a blindfold."

I MUST HAVE DOZED OFF. Early evening, and the flash of light makes me jump to my feet. Immediately I know it's not the lighthouse, but a freighter, a far-off flash of low sun on a light-colored hull. Still, this freighter is closer than any have been. I watch it, trying to figure out if I'm looking at its stern or bow. The stern. They're going away from me. But surely my radio is in range. I dive through the companionway and down into the boat.

"Can't talk right now, Mom."

I grab the radio from the chart table and scramble back out to the cockpit.

When I press the power button, the yellow battery light seems even more pallid than before. I check that the radio is set to transmit on the emergency channel. Then, with my eyes fixed on the distant freighter, I make the call.

"Mayday, mayday, mayday. This is *Mistaya*, *Mistaya*, *Mistaya*." My throat is suddenly dry. This is where I'm supposed to give my position. "Mayday. I don't know where I am. I am a small sailboat and my mom is in serious danger. Please help me."

I release the button and listen. I hear ghost voices from transmissions farther away. Nothing from the freighter. "Big ship." I'm crying now. "Please turn around."

Nothing.

"Big ship, look at your radar screen. I'm the blip behind you. My mother needs help."

The ship grows smaller in the swells, disappearing so quickly that I can imagine it is avoiding me.

"Help me. Please."

It's gone. The sun is slipping into night. And the light on the radio fades to nothing.

Maybe the battery was too low. Maybe they couldn't hear me. If they did, I wonder if they spent even a second wondering who I am.

I STARE OUT at the waves so long that my eyes feel gritty and my head hurts. For minutes at a time I watch in one direction, willing the island to appear out of the sea, then in another direction. I even look out behind the boat, as if it might suddenly burst from the waves like a submarine. I won't go below for fear of missing a glimpse of it, not even for drinking water, and by nightfall, I'm watching through a glaze of tears and I'm so exhausted that the waves all look like islands. I actually chased one, veering off course to pursue what I thought was brown land but it was water. Just water.

I should have gone below. When I finally do, Mom is awake, her eyes open, fixed, her lips parted. Circled in red, around her wound the skin is dark and blistered and crackles when I touch it. Where I touch her leg, it is dead.

TWENTY-ONE

I TURN ON EVERY LIGHT INSIDE the boat, flinging the curtains wide to send out pale beams into the dark. I switch on all our running lights and the light at the top of the mast we normally use only at anchor. If I'm sailing blind, then my only hope is to draw the attention of someone looking for me.

Will they be looking for me? Do they even care? We haven't known Emma and Mac that long. Maybe they've just shrugged us off. Maybe Jimmy and his wife are their new sailing buddies. Maybe that's how it works. Out of sight, out of mind.

Emma thinks Ty has moved on, I know she does. She might be right. Three years ago he moved on from Lindsay so fast that I didn't even realize that they'd ever been together. If he hasn't, then Jesse would say so. But she says nothing about Ty, which is like saying everything.

I guess I knew Ty would. At my going-away party, other girls were circling like vultures. It might even be Jesse that he's seeing now.

The thing about running with all the lights is that it ruins my night vision. In the cockpit all I can see is the light streaming from the boat. Everything outside of the light vanishes, which is no good since I have to watch for the light on Masamirit. If I was on the bow, in front of our light, maybe I could see better. I clip my tether onto the jack line and make my way forward.

The movement up here is enough to loosen my joints, like standing on the back of a pitching Brahma bull. I creep from one handhold to the next, keeping my weight low to offset sudden dropping waves. Finally, I reach the bow. I brace myself on the deck with my butt just in front of the headsail, my boots wedged against the toe rail. I'm wearing full foulies against the spray from the waves and the relentless wind that, at the very front of the boat, buffets me like hammers. Away from the engine noise, I can hear the waves churning under the bow. I can see better, but I have to squint against the wind to keep watch for the light.

No wonder Duncan never went forward unless he had to.

It's mesmerizing, peering into the night. Tonight, clouds cover the sky; there are no stars, no moon, just a fleece blackness and invisible sea. No light from Masamirit. And no Duncan. It amazes me that Duncan would sleep while I was alone on watch. They'd take an afternoon nap, he and Mom, and get right into bed. I'd have to wake him when my watch was done. At first, when I took the afternoon watch, I'd wake him many times: if I saw a freighter, or if the sail started to ripple, or just to ask him a question. He never minded getting woken. He said he could sleep while I was on watch because he knew I'd come and get him if I got into any trouble. He said trouble was inevitable, that there was no use worrying about it, that when it happened, we'd do all that we could to deal with it. Worry and hope, he said, they just make a sailor impatient.

How would you deal with Mom's leg wound, Duncan? Have I done everything I can? If I don't spot the Masamirit light, then she could die. Shouldn't I worry about that? Shouldn't I hope for the light?

In the density of night, I imagine black shapes appearing on the waves, the shadows of shadows, of freighters and trains, strangely, like the train that bore down on Vanessa and Bree. I can almost smell metal, the same smell as blood, repellent and exciting and it makes my stomach turn. The peapod of this boat creates a new world in the blackness. My eyes could be open or shut, and in fact I blink to make sure I'm still awake. My dream replays on the lightless stage, the one about the kiss. I shudder. Jesse said she wouldn't leave the night of my party, but she did. She said she left me in my own home, not at some stranger's place, and it wasn't her fault I passed out. She said she'd met a guy and that he wanted to leave. I shake my head to erase the dream. I rub the insides of my arms to erase the bruises of the dream. It was just a dream, and not even that. It was a memory of a dream, like a strand of cigarette smoke from a darkened window.

Cigarette smoke. I smell it again before it registers. I can smell someone's cigarette! Crazily, I look behind me to the light of the boat, but I know it can't be coming from here. I lean forward on the bowsprit, poring into the blackness. I see the red end of a cigarette arc toward the waves, then nothing.

"Hello!" My voice is ridiculously small in the wind. "Hello!"

I strain to hear. No engine noise, but someone is out here, on this one sea, a fisherman maybe, having a smoke. "I need help. Is anyone there?"

I hang over the bowsprit and I sniff sweat and dust, foreign scents that leap to my nose after days at sea. Faintly, I hear someone cough. A baby cries. And in the black sack of night I sense it more than see it, a dark more deep than the night. Another boat.

"Hey!" I shout. "Over here!"

They can see me, of course they can.

"Help me! Mayday!"

I strain to hear a response. I think I hear a man's voice, a muffled command. The baby falls abruptly silent.

Why are they running without lights? Why don't they acknowledge me? Then the night shatters and their engine starts.

"No! Don't leave me!"

I scramble back into the cockpit, let loose the headsail, and yank the wheel in the direction of the sound of their boat. For an instant, their bow appears in the circle of my light, a wooden boat so overloaded that it barely clears the waves. It's a dhow, a boat just like the pirates used.

My hands freeze on the wheel. They used no lights, no engines, because they didn't want to be detected. They had seen me and were hiding.

My throat sticks closed. What made the baby stop crying like that? In my memory I smell the metal blades of the pirates' knives. I smell Duncan's scotch, Mom's lasagna; I smell Eggman.

If I steered away now, their boat would slip past mine. They seem to be traveling south, the wind behind them. Maybe they wouldn't turn into the wind to catch me. Maybe they would let me go.

But they had every opportunity to catch me and they didn't. They didn't want to catch me. They were hiding from me, not waiting for me.

With the wheel hard over, I accelerate into their path. I can see their bow veer, but they don't have time to get out of the way. With a shuddering crunch they broadside our boat and their engine gutters and dies.

I throw the throttle down and knock the engine into neutral, then I rush to the side of the cockpit. The people on the wooden boat are making no attempt to be quiet now. I hear men shouting, and a dark face appears on their bow, shaking his fist at me.

"Please! My mother. I need help!"

His mouth is wide with anger. I can hear the sound of their engine cranking, turning over, then sputtering again.

"It's my mother. Please!"

He turns his back. Behind him, in the hollow of the boat, I can make out at least a dozen people huddled together. A woman's head scarf flaps in the wind and her hand reaches up to gather it under her chin. As the waves scrape our boats against each other and the light on the top of the mast dips toward their boat, I see that she's holding a baby to her breast. She looks up at me, her face drawn with fatigue and a worn-out desperation that's like looking in a mirror. A man beside her shouts, and she drops her head over the baby. He drops his head too just as another man steps through the huddle of people, a man with the bearing and authority and absolute control of the gunman.

I don't know where this man lives, but I speak to him in Arabic, the language of both sides of the Red Sea, words I've heard Mac use in greeting. *"As-salam alaykum."*

At first the man says nothing, then, grudgingly, he responds. *"Wa alaykum as-salam."*

I've exhausted almost my entire repertoire of the language, so using my hands, I motion to him to board our boat.

He makes a gesture that, in any language, can only mean *go to hell*, then shouts at another man who is bent over the engine. The man at the engine seems to indicate there is some problem. The man in charge yells at him, and he bends again to work on the engine.

"My mother is sick," I implore. The man ignores me.

Money. He'll help me for money. I scramble below to Mom's cabin and grab the zipper bag with our passports, credit cards and cash. I dump out everything except the cash and dash back out to the cockpit.

"My mother is sick," I repeat. Then I show him the money. "Please, help me."

He looks at the money, at the holes in the side of the boat, then he motions to a man who leaps lightly from their boat to ours.

He's younger than the others, maybe not much older than me, wearing a faded plaid shirt, pants worn thin at the knees, and knockoff Nikes. He reaches for the money, but I gesture for him to come below. The man at the engine says something and laughs. He indicates with a leer that the boy should go with me.

I lead the boy down into the boat. He stands for a moment looking dazzled, by the lights or the interior of the boat, I don't know. He seems transfixed with the torn electronics panel. I touch him on the arm and he jumps. I point to my mother in her berth.

He peers into the lee cloth, then straightens, his forehead creased. He asks me something. I point to her leg. He looks, and his breath whistles between his teeth. I say, "Please, you have to take my mother. She needs a hospital, a doctor." I'm speaking too fast. The boy steps around me, wants to leave. "No. *La.*" I grab his arm. "You must take my mother. Take her to Port Sudan."

He stops dead, and his eyes widen. He says something, but all I understand is the word *police*. Then he yanks his arm free and climbs out into the cockpit. I follow him, pulling at his pant leg. "Please don't leave me!"

He has one foot over the side when he remembers the money. He reaches out his hand. I pull back the money. I'm crying, I can't help it. "Please, you have to help me. Mayday. Please."

The man in control shouts at him or me, I can't tell. The boy hesitates. I grab the chart and gesture to me, to the sea. "At least tell me where I am."

The engine on their boat starts in a cloud of oily smoke. I jab my finger at the island on the chart. "Masamirit?" Then I cast my hand over the sea. I ask again, "Masamirit?"

"Masamirit," he says, his pronunciation different from mine. He thumbs over his shoulder and says something. All I understand is *yirmi*.

"*Yirmi*? Twenty what? Miles? Hours? Days?"

The man screams at the boy. He snatches the money out of my hand then jumps down into their boat. He indicates again the direction. "Masamirit," he says. The man cuffs him in the ear and grabs the money. The boy scrambles away. Then their engine revs up and they wallow out onto the waves. The woman with the baby watches me from under her arm as the boat slips again into darkness. I listen to it a long time until maybe I just imagine that I can hear it. Then it's gone.

I haul in the headsail so it stops its flapping and put the engine in gear. The course the boy indicated is more westerly than mine. I alter course to the west and crank the engine full on.

THREE TIMES I decide he misunderstood me and showed me the wrong way, or showed me the wrong way just because he felt like it. Three times I change back to my original heading. Three times I zig and zag across the night on his heading, on mine, sweating in my foulies, peering into the blackness for the Masamirit light. I think about the woman and child on the boat. Were they going home, or fleeing it? What was so awful about their lives that they got in that boat on a sea like this? But what can I know of the desperation of people who live along fine fluid lines of blood, religion and geography?

When it first appears, I think it must be a freighter again, just a faint white light between the darkness of sea and sky. But freighter lights don't flash, and I sail closer, close enough to count the flashes, to match the pattern with that on the chart, to know, yes, I'm looking at the light on Masamirit. I sail another mile toward it before I can no longer convince myself that I'm seeing things, then I believe it, I only just believe it; now I can reach Port Sudan. I am almost there.

TWENTY-TWO

IT'S LIKE BEING HIGH, this frenetic cocktail of exhaustion and nerves. I've followed Duncan's waypoints from the light on Masamirit, estimating actual distance where he would have used his electronics, and I'm lucky, really lucky, because with each course change, I see more freighters, more garbage in the water, more signs that I'm on track for Port Sudan. Now, an almost continuous line of tanker traffic marks a westward path in the night. If I had to, I could follow them in. But I plot each mile I make, penciling my own path on the chart, translating each hour in the cockpit to a new place on the sea, tiny steps west toward help.

Each time I go below, I hold my breath until I find my mother still with me, her heart still beating, and I tell her how close we are to landfall. "Two hours until first light, Mom." Then, "I can see it now, Mom! I can see lights on the African coastline." And finally, just as the sun burns a white line on the horizon, "Lights, Mom, from the city!"

I haven't slept, haven't eaten, don't care. I stand in the cockpit with my eyes on the distant city, plotting the chart with certainty, now that I can take bearings from landmarks. My penciled line creeps closer toward Port Sudan, and I'm grateful for it because just looking at the far-off city isn't real enough.

I've notched up our speed and the sound of the engine hums through my feet and legs until I feel like I'm more part of the boat than the world. I stand at the wheel and steer, imagining that I'm steering a knife-edge course, trying to believe that I'm getting us there faster.

It's been hours since I first spotted the city and now, finally, it emerges in focus. I can make out the white-pillared oil tanker station, a city in itself, and from that, and Duncan's notes on the chart, the course to find the harbor entrance. At this point, I could plunk us against almost any hard place on the shoreline, even the tanker pontoons, but I know where I need to go to get the fastest help for my mother. I have to find *Pandanus*.

With one hand on the wheel, one on the chart, I visually navigate a line toward the coastline, marking radio towers and mosque domes and water towers, matching the icons on the chart with what I can actually see, marking my progress toward the basin where sailboats would dock. I call to my mother from the cockpit, "Just five more miles. We'll be there in time for breakfast." Then, from behind a massive stone breakwater, "I see sticks, Mom! I can see the masts of boats!"

I've shrugged off my jacket and fleece, but I'm still in my foulie pants and boots. Sweat is running down my legs. I flip on the automatic steering and unearth two rubber fenders from the cockpit locker. These I tie onto the rail on the side of the boat to cushion the boat from the dock. Then I scramble to attach a line at the stern and the bow of the boat, and one in the middle to hold us to the dock. I jump back into the cockpit just as the boat reaches the opening in the breakwater.

I throttle down and ease the boat into the harbor. Instantly, the sea flattens and the wind dies in my ears, the scent of land fills my nose. I hear cars and the sounds of halyards clanking against masts. A huge lump lodges in my throat and I have to work hard not to cry. I can't cry. Not now, not yet.

Boats are tied along several concrete pontoons. It's early, and I don't see anyone in the cockpits. I see flags from Sweden and the Netherlands, many flags, but I stop myself from searching for *Pandanus* and look for a place to tie up. Any place will do, even against another boat. But there's a vacant spot on the very end of one pontoon, and this is what I aim for.

Boats don't have brakes, and it's not pretty. I crunch the boat against the pontoon, popping the fenders back onto the deck, scraping fiberglass against concrete, the engine roaring in reverse to stop us. Now several heads emerge from their boats. I kill the engine, grab the spring line at the middle of the boat and leap over the rail onto the pontoon. The sudden hardness of land makes my knees buckle and I stumble, but I manage to loop the line over a cleat and snug *Mistaya* to the pontoon. The bow is yawing, but the boat isn't going anywhere. People are running now; I hear feet pounding on concrete coming toward me, voices calling. I'm on my knees, struggling to get to my feet. "Help." It comes out as a croak. "Help!" Now I'm crying. A bare-chested man lifts me, speaks to me in a German accent. I indicate the boat. "My mother!" Another man jumps aboard *Mistaya*, tosses the bow and stern lines to others now on the pontoon. "My mother! You have to help my mother!"

"Lib!"

I hear Emma and now I can't stand. The German man catches me, lowers me to the concrete. Emma is running, her eyes on me, the boat, the shreds of mainsail bound on the boom, the bullet holes, her eyes taking it all in. I motion to the boat. "My mother."

Without breaking stride, Emma points to a woman on the pontoon. "Get us a vehicle. No, two, an ambulance if you can." The woman's eyes widen and she stands, dazed. "Now!" The woman blinks, then moves off toward the ramp. "Run!" The woman runs. Emma vaults onto *Mistaya* and disappears below.

The German man is holding my hand, talking to me. I don't have a clue what he's saying, but I hang on his words.

Emma sticks her head out of the companionway, orders more people around, glances once at me, then ducks below again. I try to get up, to go to my mother, but my knees are liquid, and the German man cluck-clucks, tells me to sit. Several men return with gangplanks and lengths of rope and proceed to lash together a stretcher. They hoist this onto the deck of *Mistaya* and lower it down the companionway.

Then Mac's hands are on my shoulders, his voice soft and solid in my ears. "Duncan?"

I can't form the words, so I shake my head. His hands seem very still, then he squeezes my shoulders. "You did well, girl." He leaves me to help with the stretcher.

Someone slips a blanket around me even though I'm sweating, because that's what you do for people who are bashed up, I guess. The German man helps me to my feet and leads me to a laundry van, waiting at the top of the ramp. The woman is there, the one who Emma told to get the ambulance, and she climbs into the front seat with me. She's talking to me, saying something about the van being faster than waiting for an ambulance, but I'm not listening. I'm watching Mac and the other men carry Mom on the stretcher. They're running. They slide the stretcher in on the floor of the van; Mac jumps in and shouts something at the driver. I see the driver for the first time, his eyes wide with concern. At Mac's command, the driver steps on the gas and we lurch into the street.

Mom's eyes are closed, and I watch Mac beside her on the floor of the van, grateful that he's there, that he's urging the driver on, that he doesn't have all the time in the world because she's sick, my mother, very, very sick. Sick and not dead. The woman puts her arm around me, and I put my head on her shoulder. She speaks to me like I'm a child, words without meaning, but I want to believe her. "You're going to be okay."

TWENTY-THREE

I PEEL ANOTHER ORANGE, letting the juice run down into my shirtsleeves, licking the juice from the side of my hand, eating the orange in exploding mouthfuls. Mac peels one for my mother and places small pieces on a plate beside her bed. She lifts these to her mouth and chews slowly.

Mac is just back from Tel Aviv. He finished the delivery of the *Pandanus* while Emma stayed with Mom and me.

In the hospital in Port Sudan, Mom got massive doses of antibiotics, then an air ambulance took her here to the capital, Khartoum, for surgery to cut the dead tissue out of her leg. The doctor took as little as he could. He said he used to be a military doctor, that gunshot wounds often get infected, especially if they're not treated right away. He said Mom was lucky she was shot with an AK-47, that an AK-47 is actually designed to wound, not kill. I said, "How humane," but then he explained that it's better to wound a soldier than kill him. That way the soldier is taken out of the fighting along with other soldiers who have to carry him.

I guess a Sudanese doctor knows something about war.

The doctor said that Mom's concussion was only minor but that she might have trouble remembering what happened. He figures it was her blood loss that kept her so out of it. He said she's lucky.

I'VE BEEN TELLING Mom the story again about that last night at sea, finding my way to Port Sudan.

"It was Duncan's chart that got us there. He had the course changes marked right into the harbor."

"That's always the hardest part of a passage," Mom says. "Leaving the fairway of the open sea and heading for the rocks. Duncan was like a cat, the last part of a passage." Her smile fades. The silence around her bed grows.

Then Mac speaks. "I thought you were delayed because of the storm, that you'd lost your mast or something. But then when we couldn't reach you on the radio, I knew it was something more."

"That storm," Emma shudders. "We never should have left port."

Mac says, "The storm surprised everyone, even the forecasters. We were deep in it, and Djibouti Weather was still calling for calm winds. No one could have anticipated that it would hit us that way."

Jimmy lost his mast in the storm and he and his wife got airlifted off the boat, abandoning it. Emma says the boat washed into a bay still trailing its rigging but otherwise, not a scratch on it. Jimmy and his wife were already long gone home.

Just to Emma I say, "I'm glad for the storm."

Emma nods. She knows about Eggman.

"Search planes couldn't find you," Mac says. "The storm must have blown you miles off course." Mac chews and swallows another half-orange. "How you got so close to Masamirit on your own is mind-boggling."

Officially, Duncan is missing at sea and presumed dead. Mac said that on his trip to the Suez in *Pandanus*, a little bird landed on his boat too, a bird with yellow breast feathers. Mom wants to have a funeral for Duncan when we get home, buy a headstone, put it on an empty grave. But we've scattered his ashes, all of us, on the Red Sea.

I say to Mom, "I e-mailed Dad today. He wants to come and take us home." My throat sticks on the word *us*. "I meant to say, he wants to take me home. Although, I guess you could tag along."

"We should have quite the entourage." Mom's sister wants to come, and my grandfather, and about nine of Mom's friends, including a dentist and a professional dancer. Strange but true. Mom sighs, "It'll be good to be home."

Home. Our house is still leased to tenants, so we're going to stay with Mom's sister. She has a condo downtown that looks onto English Bay. I can take the bus to my school, or I might enroll in a new one.

Emma and Mac will bring *Mistaya* through the Suez for us. They found a charter boat company in the Caribbean, that will put *Mistaya* in its fleet, and offered to deliver it there for us. They'll fit it in around their other deliveries, sail through the Mediterranean to the Atlantic and cross with it in December, just after hurricane season.

Selling *Mistaya* wasn't an option, not even for Mom. She says *Mistaya* is part of Duncan, part of all of us, and she can't let it go. The charter company will take care of the boat for her, and we can still sail on it a few weeks each year. I'm not sure Mom is eager to sail again. It's maybe too soon for her.

I say to her, "Dad doesn't need to come. I think I can find the way."

Mom smiles. "You could, I know that. But let him be a father."

I'M PACKING MOM's bag as she sits with her leg up, watching me. I've already packed mine. There wasn't much I could take. Everything seems to match a boat life, not a back-home life, although I did take the knife Dad gave me. Into Mom's bag I put her things, and a few of Duncan's. I unzip his shaving kit and breathe in his familiar smell. She says, "It's hard, this goodbye." I glance at her, thinking she's talking about Duncan. "I mean leaving our life on *Mistaya*," she says.

She hasn't been back to the boat. It's in dry dock in Port Sudan getting the holes in the hull fixed. Mac took me back for a few days to collect our things. Mac and I talked for hours, about important things, like friends talk. Real friends. He knows about loss, Mac does. And when it was time to leave the boat, I did cry. I zip up Duncan's case and tuck it in Mom's bag.

She says, "You must be looking forward to seeing your friends. Jesse. Ty."

"No. Not Ty," I say too quickly, too loudly.

She's silent for a moment, then says, "Because of the party?"

I know what she wants. She wants me to tell her that I was totally innocent, that Ty forced me into that bedroom, into that bed, that I could press charges. I may not remember much of the party, but I wouldn't have refused Ty. I never did, even if I wanted to. It was the price of being with Ty, a price I paid from the very start. I say to her, "I'm done with Ty. It just took me a while to see."

She nods. "You're a different person now."

"Maybe I was a different person then. Now, I'm just me."

Her eyes slide downward and her eyebrows knot. I say, "You don't have to be afraid for me. I survived Ty." She starts to say something, but I cut her off. I know that she's thinking about the pirates. "I'm not afraid for you, either, after what happened on *Mistaya*. We survived that too."

"But if I hadn't fired the flare gun…"

"It might not have made a difference. If I'd been up on deck with you, maybe I could have helped."

"Or maybe you would have been shot too. We never should have left port. I was too anxious to go."

"I made us late, Mom." Just saying it makes my guts drop. "I put us in the path of both the pirates and the storm."

"The storm hit everyone, Lib. And the pirates might have found us anyway."

"But we were alone. I'm sorry, Mom. I'm sorry about Duncan. I'm sorry for everything."

She's crying now, and I let her be. The pirates blew a hole in her life; I never used a gun, but I leveled some emotionally lethal shots, at her and at myself. Her leg will heal faster than her heart.

DAD MET ME in Cairo even though I told him he didn't have to. He said he's always wanted to see the Egyptian pyramids. He showed up in full Tilley gear and brand-new safari boots. I suggested we go by camel to the pyramids but just the thought turned him green. We rode in a tour bus, air-conditioned, and sat right at the front.

TWENTY-FOUR

I FLIP CLOSED MY MATH textbook and toss it and my note-book into my pack. I yawn, stretch, check the kitchen clock. Eleven. I'm almost caught up on my courses and just in time for June finals. I won't exactly make the Principal's List, but I probably won't have to repeat anything. I decided to go to a school close to my aunt's condo. Technically, it's an *inner city* school so it should have drugs, gangs and violence. Maybe it does. For me, going to this school was just easier.

Jesse thinks I have the best life, living downtown. She'd like to stay with me on weekends, but I'm sleeping on the couch in my aunt's living room, so there's truly no room for her. I've gone to her place a few times, but we don't have much to talk about anymore. It's easier to go to Dad's and rent a movie, something good and scary.

Ty called me when I got back, but I said I was busy with my mom. She's taking a photography course and works out in a physio gym for her leg. And she writes in her journal for hours. She's taking care of herself. I could have told Ty that he was an anal orifice, but this was just easier. He wouldn't get it, anyway.

Mom comes into the kitchen, sets her tea mug on the counter. "There's an e-mail from Emma. They're finishing a delivery to Palma in a couple of weeks, then they'll bring *Mistaya* into the Mediterranean."

"I know, Mom. Emma e-mailed me too."

I watch Mom as she moves around the small kitchen, putting away the kettle, wiping the counter. She limps, probably always will. She says, "The summer is slow for deliveries, everyone using their boats, so they'll be able to take their time sailing the Mediterranean." She glances at me, then scrubs something on the counter that I can't see.

I say, "And Mac wants to spend some time scuba diving in Egypt."

Scrub, scrub. "That's right," she says. "In the Red Sea."

She's going to wear the counter right through. "Mom." Her hand pauses on the sponge and she looks up at me. I say, "Are you okay?"

She puts the sponge on the side of the sink, wipes her hands, folds the dishtowel over the bar on the oven. "What else did Emma write to you?"

Ah. I take a breath. "She asked if I wanted to come and sail with them for the summer." Mom crosses her arms, uncrosses them, then she jams her hands in her jeans pockets. "But I told her that I couldn't."

"Why?"

"Because I might have to do summer school."

"But you won't have to."

"Because I'm thinking of getting a summer job."

"Since when?"

"Since right now." I cross my arms. "Can we drop this?"

She crosses her arms. "You're not going because of me."

"No."

"You think you need to take care of me."

Eye roll. "No."

"I don't need you to take care of me. I can look after myself."

"I know that."

"So, why won't you go?"

"I told you."

Eye roll. "No. What are you afraid of?"

"I'm not afraid. Why are you trying to get rid of me?"

"I'm not." She sighs. "Do you want to go?"

"Maybe."

"Then why don't you?"

I tap my pencil on the table. She reaches over, puts her hand on mine, silences the pencil. Again she asks, "Why?"

I feel tears coming. "I'm not sure I can. God. I'm not sure I can be so far away." From you.

"You're just an airplane ticket away." Then, quietly, "You've been so much farther away." She's studying me, like she's taking a picture and the camera is very slow. "You should go."

I nod.

She leans down, wraps her arms around me. I inhale her mother-scent. She says, "Sometimes you have to be far from home to find what makes you free." She gives me a squeeze. "Go."

TWENTY-FIVE

MISTAYA IS BACK IN THE WATER, bobbing in a slip in the marina at Port Sudan, her hull fixed and sail replaced. Emma patrols the deck, inspecting the rigging hardware. From a deck fitting, she extracts a wisp of the old mainsail and hands it to me.

"Souvenir."

I take it from her and release it on the wind. "Do you think she'll be okay on her own?"

"Your mother? What do you think?"

I shrug, become very busy checking a non-existent spot on the rail.

She says, "I'll tell you what I know of your mother. She's brave, smart and resourceful. And she wants what is best for you. Your being here doesn't change what you have with your mother. It's the relationship that's important, the connection." She fixes me with a stare. "You're choosing a path. That's not the same as running away. I know the difference."

WE'VE HAD NEW cushions made for the boat and these fit snugly on the benches. Over the last couple of weeks I took everything out of the shelves and lockers, cleaned them, then arranged them neatly. I sanded the scratches out of the dining table, polished the woodwork until it gleamed, filled the water and fuel tanks.

I bought a new go-bag, red, just like the last one. Now I inspect the contents: flashlights, batteries, food, water. A GPS. Antibiotics. All double-bagged. I pick up the photographs I've selected, three individual shots. There's one of Mom I took at the airport. I made her sister get out of the picture. Mom's hand is lifted part way, like she's starting to wave, her mouth is smiling but her eyes can't. I'll miss her too. The picture of Duncan is one Mom took a few years ago when they were hiking in the Rockies. He looks perfectly happy, but the reason I chose the picture is the birds in the background, a flock of plain little birds, hovering on the wind like tiny sails. The third photo is me, a new one, taken on the bow of *Mistaya* when we put her back in the water. I look perfectly happy too.

All the photos I bag, and bag again, then slip them into the go-bag with the other items. The last thing I put in is a sealed container of sand for Fanny the cat. We've rigged her a swinging sea berth, but she likes to sleep on my bed.

Emma had me check the oil level and batteries, and I see her back there now, double-checking my work, but that's fine with me. She's the captain. Mac calls from the cockpit, "Are you two about ready to cast off?"

I glance at my watch, Mom's watch really, but she wanted me to have it, and make a note on the chart of our departure time. I strap the go-bag into place next to the companion-way, grab my hat and sunglasses and climb out into the cockpit. Emma follows me, leaps down onto the pontoon to untie our lines.

"Take us out," she calls to me as she throws Mac the line and climbs back on board.

And I do.

Diane Tullson spent over a year traveling some of the same waters as Libby does in *Red Sea*. While not attacked by pirates, Diane and her family lived with the knowledge that the danger was real and they were a long way from home. Diane is also the author of *Saving Jasey* (Orca, 2002). Diane lives in Vancouver, British Columbia. *www.dianetullson.com*

Also by Diane Tullson

Saving Jasey

Confronting his family's cruelty and his friend's fear of a deadly disease, Gavin learns that life is often unfair.

Thirteen-year-old Gavin's home life is far from perfect. His older brother is a bully, his father has no time for him and his mother hasn't been the same since she hit a pig on the highway. Gavin finds sanctuary in his friend Trist McVeigh's seemingly perfect home. His blossoming infatuation with Trist's older sister Jasey helps fill the emotional void. But all is not as it seems in the McVeigh home. Trist's uncle suffers from Huntington's disease, a devastating degenerative brain disorder that may have been the reason for the suicide of Trist's father. Is Grandpa Jack also affected? And if so, are Trist and Jasey also in danger? Unable to deal with the threat of a potential illness, Jasey starts to self-destruct and she becomes involved with the worst kind of people. While trying to understand the dramatic changes in her personality, Gavin finds that the threat of a silent killer like Huntington's disease is as damaging as a corrosive family life. Gavin decides to do what he can to save Jasey and, ultimately, save himself.